# OWEN AND ADDY: A RED TEAM WEDDING NOVELLA

## THE RED TEAM, BOOK 14

## ELAINE LEVINE

Published by Elaine Levine
Copyright © 2018 Elaine Levine
Last Updated: June 20, 2018
Cover art by The Killion Group, Inc.
Editing by Arran McNicol @ editing720
Proofing by Carol Agnew @ Attention to Detail Proofreading

Print ISBNs:
ISBN-13: 978-1721272822
ISBN-10: 1721272828

## OWEN AND ADDY: A RED TEAM WEDDING NOVELLA - BLURB

Writing love letters to a dead woman was the sum total of Owen Tremaine's romantic prospects without Addy Jacobs in his life.

When he learned she was still alive, and that she'd suffered far worse than a broken heart, he had to fight to regain her trust and convince her he wasn't part of the machinations  by friend and foe alike—that had put them through hell.

So much has changed in the decade he and Addy lost —but their love never died. Owen's learning to be a father to her boys—one of them his own son. They're putting the pieces of their lives back together, beginning at the point they left off.

And now it's time for the wedding their enemies denied them so long ago, but can Owen put her dreams ahead of his fears when it comes to a dangerous choice they have to make?

Length: Approximately 140 pages

Ages: 18 & up (story contains sex, profanity, and violence)

Owen and Addy: A Red Team Wedding Novella (The Red Team, Book 14) is part of a serialized story that includes nine full-length novels and nine wedding novellas. This series is best read in order, starting with The Edge of Courage.

Join the conversation on Facebook: Visit Elaine Levine's War Room - http://geni.us/hxFk to talk about this book and all of her suspenseful stories!

# OTHER BOOKS BY ELAINE LEVINE

(This series may be read in any order.)

# DEDICATION

*For Barry, my own beacon of light.*

## A NOTE FROM THE AUTHOR

.

We begin *Owen and Addy* at the point where Max & Hope: A Red Team Wedding Novella left off. To maximize your enjoyment of this serialized story, I highly recommend reading the series in order, starting with *The Edge of Courage* and including the Red Team wedding novellas, before beginning this book!

And make sure you never miss a book from me by signing up for my new release announcements at http://geni.us/GAlUjx.

—Elaine

## WHEN WE LAST VISITED THE RED TEAM...

Here's a refresher for those of you who have read the previous Red Team books (skip this and go read them if you haven't yet!). This is where we left our heroes...

### ***** Spoilers! *****

- Owen found Addy Jacobs, his long-lost love.
- Owen met the son he never knew about, as well as Addy's second son.
- Addy and the boys are living with Owen at the team's headquarters.
- Owen has reconnected with his childhood friend and recent nemesis, Wendell (Jax) Jacobs.
- Lion and his pride are with the team at Blade's house.
- Ivy and Mandy are about six months pregnant.
- Jason Parker and Cecil Edwards are dead.
- The Omnis have temporarily been run to ground.
- Wynn's parents, Joyce and Nathan Ratcliff, and Owen's dad, Nick Tremaine, have all

been altered by gene modification procedures, as has Addy.

- Max and Hope are still on their honeymoon bike run.
- Something mysterious is still stalking the team.
- It's early January at the Tremaine Headquarters in Wyoming.

And now, we continue with **Owen** and **Addy's** wedding novella…

# 1

—————

Owen Tremaine stared at the paperwork in front of him, seeing none of it. He and his team had been onsite for less than a year, and already four of his teammates had gotten married. Max was still out on his honeymoon. None of that was what he'd been expecting when he pulled the group together and came out here. Kit and Rocco were going to be dads again in a few months. Hell, Owen was sitting at the very desk where he'd written love letters to a dead woman.

But Adelaide Jacobs was no longer a figment of his lost past. She was his now, in flesh and blood; only logistics were keeping them from sharing the same last name.

It was their turn to tie the knot. He was done waiting.

He checked his phone to find her. She was in the

new greenhouse that Blade had the construction crew build while they were there working on the basement.

Owen went outside via the French doors in his office and crossed the lawn. The day was crisp but mild for an early January morning in Wyoming. The greenhouse sat near the caretaker's house that Jim and Russ lived in. It was a huge monstrosity of a glass dome and reminded Owen of the conservatory at Addy's mountain house. She'd naturally gravitated toward it—not because she missed anything about her old place, but because she liked getting her hands dirty in a garden.

A wall of moist, hot air wrapped around him when he stepped inside. Fans created an artificial breeze, rustling the leaves of the banana and lemon trees.

Addy looked up and smiled. He'd never thought to have her back in his life, yet here she was, beautiful and thriving, like the plants she tended.

Today was the day.

"Look"—she lifted a heavy leaf on a vine to show him something growing out of its faded flower—"we have baby zucchinis starting. And the butter lettuce is almost ready for harvesting." She hurried to another area in the big greenhouse and held her hand under the framework of a strawberry bed that somehow had the berries hanging upside down. "The boys planted these a few weeks ago and the strawberries are already starting."

Owen smiled at the wonder in her eyes. She spent

a lot of her days in here, working on the indoor farm for the household. He pulled her into his arms. "I need to talk to you."

Worry flashed across her face, but she hid it with a smile as she set her hands on his arms. "Okay."

"When can I make you Mrs. Tremaine?"

She relaxed. "That's up to you. We could go get our marriage license tomorrow. Then we could go to the justice of the peace anytime. I don't want to make this a big deal. I get a little panicky thinking about having another wedding ceremony."

"We can make it low-key, but I want to have that first dance with you, so it needs to be more than a run to the JP. I used to play that dance with you through my head, pretend what it would have been like, before I lost you. That was my go-to daydream when things were stressful."

She rubbed his arms. "I know. You wrote about that in one of your letters to me."

"And I'd like my dad and your brother to be with us. Jax needs to walk you down the aisle. Let's find out when they can get back here."

"This is sounding like a big deal."

"Not really. Just family."

"And team and cubs."

"Which is just family."

"Maybe we could all go out to Mama Rosa's for supper to celebrate. Make it easy on everyone here."

"Or we could have them cater it for us here. I don't want you stressing about this. We can hire an event group to do the whole thing. Setup. Take-down. Cleanup. Decorations. Music. All of it."

"That's a lot of money."

"Not for our wedding. And it's less stress on the team, especially since they're still recovering from the last wedding." He smiled at Addy, hoping to ease the tension rolling in waves from her. "Now what about wedding rings?"

She actually flushed a little. "I was looking through Hope's wedding magazines and found a jeweler I like in Denver. They have just the ring I want."

He smiled, warmed to learn she'd been thinking about their wedding. "And what does this ring look like?"

"It's an emerald-cut aquamarine with two diamond baguettes."

"An aquamarine as a center stone? Not a diamond?"

"Cecil gave me a diamond. I don't want that again. Besides, the aquamarine reminds me of your eyes, so having it with me all the time is like having you with me."

"I like that." He sighed. "I can't believe I'm going to suggest this...but why don't you pick out some wedding dress photos from those magazines and give them to Val? He can have his friend who owns the bridal shop source them and bring them up for you to try on. The other ladies may want to pick something out too. She can bring all of that up for you to select from."

"I didn't want to make such a big deal out of this."

"It is a big deal. It's our wedding. I want it to be amazing. I want it to wipe out any memory you have of your first ceremony, which wasn't a wedding at all, but it's holding that spot in your head."

"Nothing about that day was good. Nothing. I try not to think about it at all." Her blue eyes deepened, in that odd way they had of changing with her emotions, a side effect of her modifications.

"Use our wedding to purge that from your mind."

She nodded slowly, mulling it over. "Okay. I will." She wrapped her arms around his waist. "Is there anything you specifically want included or excluded? A meal or cake preference? Colors or themes?"

"I just want my dance with you. Everything else is gravy."

OWEN CALLED Jax on his walk back to the house. "Hey," he said when the call was picked up.

"Owen. Your dad's here with me. I've got you on speaker. S'up?"

"Dad."

"Son."

Perfunctory greetings done, Owen cut to the issue. "Wynn phoned her folks and asked them to come back. They said they couldn't until you gave them approval."

"Which I didn't give," Jax said, "for reasons I'm sure you can understand, given the circumstances."

"I need them here."

"Tell me about the situation you've going on there," Jax said. "Something about an invisible intruder?"

"Yeah. Someone or something has been physically accessing the house. Can't catch him on camera—he interferes with electronics. Cameras aside, he's able to hide himself somehow. We could walk right past him and not know it."

"That's why I stashed the Ratcliffs," Jax said. "There are things we don't know about, things we've only heard about through gossip and anecdotal evidence. The urban legends that are growing around these human modifications indicate these changed beings are capable of extra-human behaviors."

"Can you do unusual things, Dad?" Owen asked.

"Not that I know of. I was changed in a lab environment where the doctors monitoring me were trying to establish a control against which the physiology of other changed beings could be measured. I'm about to start my training. I will say that I do have urges and impulses, intuitions that I didn't have—or wasn't aware of—before being altered."

"Have either of you heard of a man called Bastion?" Owen asked. "He speaks French." Silence. A big, pregnant silence.

"Is that who's been coming to your headquarters?" Jax asked.

"I believe so. At least, that's how he introduced himself to one of our team members."

"We know some things about the study in which he was modified. He's part of a group the Ratcliffs had in their sights."

"Had?" Owen asked.

"Yeah. The study went on for a long while," Nick said, "but ultimately imploded, and its participants, including Bastion, got lost over time. He's one of a small group of men who were changed then sent to work for a private military consulting firm that operates in South America and the Middle East several years ago. Lethal motherfuckers, Owen."

"After their modifications, half the company went bad, half stayed good," Jax added. "It's unclear which half he's on."

"Bastion's in a group led by a guy named Liege," Nick said. "We don't know their legal names. They called themselves Liege's Legion. We don't know much about this group. It appeared they'd broken apart and had gone their separate ways. Rumor has it that Liege and several of his men are here in the U.S., but we haven't been able to substantiate that yet. If it's true, they may be getting the band back together."

"'Several' men isn't much of a legion," Owen said.

"Considering they can operate as effectively as a

unit ten times their size, they're enough as they are," Nick said.

"Why are they here?" Owen asked.

"That's unknown at this point," Jax said. "We think they're after the scientists who changed them."

"Was that the Ratcliffs?" Owen asked.

"No." Sounded as if Nick had moved closer to the phone. "But the Ratcliffs have the broadest knowledge about these human modifications and the players involved. And they're some of the last researchers the Omnis haven't yet terminated. Plus, they're well connected in Omni scientific circles. Even if the scientists responsible for the Legion's enhancements have been ended, the Ratcliffs may be able to recover their research."

"I need talk to the them so I can learn how to deal with these guys," Owen said. "What are their known capabilities?"

"They each have different skills and strengths," Nick said, "but all of them have enhanced mental abilities that allow them to manipulate physical things and mental conditions in those they encounter. Bastion is thought to have enhanced abilities around telepathy and electromagnetic projection."

"How is that possible?"

"We're still learning," Nick said. "These enhancements are proof regular humans are capable of far more than science has even speculated. It's thought this group was given several doses of nanos programmed to modify neural networks, giving them access to their full capabilities, basically rewiring their brains for maximum use. The range of abilities of Liege's Legion isn't fully known. We suspect they can utilize a psychic network, which is intensified by the number of warriors in their mental network."

"If I were you, Owen," Jax said, "I'd relocate. Fast."

"That's not going to happen," Owen said. "We have families here, kids starting school soon, wives with businesses. Our lives are here."

"And the Legion's found you. You're fucked if you stay there. I can give you safe harbor. All of you."

"Like you did with the other prides Ace sent your way?"

"Exactly."

"Good to know." Owen sighed, packing that info away for a future discussion. "You said the Ratcliffs might be able to get a hold of the research this Legion is looking for. Make that happen. With that in hand, we at least have some leverage."

"Roger," Jax said. "I'll put a team on it."

"Good, because in other news," Owen said, "Addy and I are getting married, hopefully before the end of this month. We'd like you here for that."

"I'm happy for you, son," Nick said.

"Pretty damned short notice, bro," Jax grumbled.

"Couldn't help that," Owen said. "The timing just worked out for us to do this now."

"Of course we'll come out," Nick said. "Thanks

for including us. Let us know when you have a firm date."

"Addy wants Jax to walk her down the aisle."

"Fine. We'll be there," Jax said.

"And while you're here, we can have a chat with my team about the Legion and what our options are."

"It'll be a short chat, 'cause you only have two choices: either take the modifications and go into hiding while you adjust to them, or get out of the fight altogether. There is no middle ground in this."

Neither of those choices were real options. Owen ended the call.

He and his team were good at what they did, but they weren't good enough to fight a group of men like Bastion, whose skills made his crew look as if they were playing a game of tag in the middle of a busy freeway.

ADDY FINISHED up in the greenhouse as quickly as she could. She filled a basket with the produce she'd harvested for the day. After she took it in to Russ in the kitchen, she washed her hands and went into the living room. She was jumping out of her skin, dying to share her news with someone. She didn't have to wait long; Mandy was the second person to come for the noon meal.

"I'm so glad I'm not the first person here," Mandy said, smiling. "I already hit Russ up for a snack an hour ago. They're going to start deducting a food stipend from Rocco's pay before this pregnancy is over."

Addy laughed. "How are you feeling?"

"Right now? Starved." Mandy chuckled. "Over-all, though, not bad for a first pregnancy and knowing nothing at all about what to expect." She tilted her head as she studied Addy. "You look awfully happy."

"Owen and I are getting married. I mean, we knew we would, but he wants to set a date."

Mandy let out a shout of delight and hugged her. "That's wonderful news! I'm so happy for you both. And the boys. This will be great for them."

Addy, still holding Mandy's hands, nodded vigor-ously. "Sometimes it's hard to understand how every-thing has turned around for us. I'd given up on him and my dreams and any kind of a future that I wanted. And now this."

"Oh, stop it." Mandy pulled her hands free to wipe her eyes. "You're going to make me cry. I cry at everything now. You're just proof that miracles do happen. And since we've been through so many weddings already, we're expert at doing them. We'll have to get with the others and put a plan together."

"I'd love that. Owen wants us to hire a wedding planner to do most of the work, just to make it easier on everyone."

"Not necessary. We can do it—but, of course, it's your choice."

"We'll talk. I think I do want to go that route, but

it still means I need a lot of help selecting a planner and making different choices of things."

"What date where you thinking of?"

"We'll set one as soon as we find an event planner who can do it quickly. A couple of weeks? Three, maybe?"

"That could be tight for a planner, but we'll help you find one who can take it on. Ivy knows a lot of them."

"Ivy knows a lot of what?" Ivy asked as she came into the living room.

"Addy and Owen are getting married as soon as possible and want to hire a wedding planner," Mandy replied.

Ivy's whole face brightened as she turned to Addy. "You guys are ready to set a date?"

Addy laughed and nodded as Ivy hugged her.

"Oh, we have so much to do!" Ivy said.

"We don't want this be a burden," Addy said. "We're hoping the event planner can take most of it on."

"But we still have to settle on decorations, menus, dresses—all of it!" Ivy stopped and gave Addy a wary glance. "You will let us help you, won't you?"

"Yes. Please. We'll decide what we need to, then hand it over to the planner to execute."

"When were you wanting to do this?" Ivy asked.

"ASAP," Mandy said, chuckling as she linked her arm through Addy's.

"Owen suggested having Val's friend bring up

some options for our dresses," Addy said. "So after we settle on a wedding planner, I think that would be the next step. And then Owen and I have to go shopping for rings, but I think I found the one I want."

"Did you?" Mandy asked, excitement in her eyes. "What does it look like?"

"I'll show you." Addy went over to a stack of magazines that still sat on top of one of the side tables in the living room. She was glad Jim hadn't cleared them away—he'd seen her looking at them several times. She grabbed the one with the jeweler's ad. "Here it is."

"Ohhh. Very nice. And they have a store in Boulder."

"Right." Addy nodded.

"You could borrow my aquamarine necklace and earrings—knock out something borrowed and something blue at the same time!" Ivy offered.

"Well, whenever you're ready to go down there," Mandy said, "just let us know. We can take care of the boys."

Addy looked into Mandy's green eyes as a stunning realization hit her: she had friends. Real friends —people who hadn't known her before a couple of months ago but who would drop what they were doing to help in any way that they could. How rare and wonderful was that?

"Thank you."

Others came into the room then, and each was given the news. Hugs and chatter and happy tears were everywhere. In the midst of the mayhem, she looked up to see Owen watching her with his somber eyes. Seeing her, a smile eased his expression.

He crossed the room and pulled her into his arms. "Jax will be coming out for the wedding."

"That's good news. So why the worried face?"

He shook his head then kissed her forehead. "That's just my resting happy face. You know. For show."

OWEN WENT BACK to work in the den after lunch. He nodded at Kelan, the last of the group to come through on their way to the bunker.

Kelan paused before leaving the room. "Hey—I wanted to say congrats to you. I'm glad you and Addy are getting married. Do you know when the wedding's going to be?"

"We're still talking about that."

"Have you written your vows?"

"No. I have to write vows?" Owen frowned. He caught the shift in Kelan's demeanor. "Fucking tell me, K. Is there something I'm supposed to do that I don't know about?"

"Your wedding is your wedding. It isn't for me to tell you how to do it."

Owen sighed, then came around his desk to lean against its edge. "No, it isn't. But you have an opinion?"

Kelan made a face as if he was hesitant to say anything. "Ceremonies are important, Owen. We don't go through life alone—our ancestors and spirit guides travel through it with us. Our ceremonies deliver important messages to them."

Owen crossed his arms. "I don't know my ancestors. Or about any spirit guides."

"Yes, you do. Our research into the Omnis has uncovered much about them and their place in the resistance. You are the son, grandson, and great-grandson of fighters. You are what you are because they were what they were. Your wedding honors them as much as it does you and Addy. This is not a casual occasion."

"Shit."

"And Addy has been through hell."

"As have I without her."

"Mm-hmm, but you're a warrior. It's your job to carry hell on your shoulders."

Owen sighed and rubbed the space between his eyes. "So what do I do?"

"You write the words that speak from your heart to hers. And you say them in front of us to show her how you honor her, to show her that we also honor her."

Owen nodded at the wide leather cuffs that Kelan wore on his wrists. "You haven't made your vows public."

"No, because the claiming ceremony was between

me and Fiona. When we marry, we'll share our public vows."

Owen held Kelan's gaze. "So I have to make a show out of this wedding."

"It isn't a show, it's a reveal. You bare your soul to her and she to you. And we are your witnesses. I'd help you with this, but only you can come up with what you wish to reveal. It's your words and your emotions—it's all you. And all Addy."

"Okay. I'll give it some thought."

Kelan gave Owen a sympathetic smile, then left him alone in the office. Owen considered his advice. He couldn't really argue with Kelan. He didn't know about the ancestors part, but he did agree that Addy deserved a day honoring her.

Hell, she deserved a lifetime of being honored.

## 2

A ddy was overwhelmed at how fast things were moving forward with her and Owen's wedding. With Ivy's help, they'd hired an event planner that was able to make things happen in just weeks. It helped that they were past the holiday wedding season and still well before the major spring season.

All the logistical decisions had been made and the planner was progressing well with the project. Addy couldn't wait to see it all come together.

Val's friend had come up with two vans full of dress and accessory choices for them. Among the offerings, Addy found her perfect dress. The seamstress she'd brought with her had adjusted it for her during the same visit, which made the whole process so much easier.

Addy had considered getting tuxes for Augie and Troy, but Augie wanted to wear the same outfit the cubs were wearing—a blue blazer, white shirt, and khakis. And, of course, since Augie was wearing that, Troy wanted to wear his. That made their attire something simple to handle.

Addy and Owen were finally about to head to Denver to meet with the jeweler she'd selected. She'd barely been able to sleep for the excitement. She went outside to find him waiting for her next to one of the team's SUVs.

She smiled as she stood next to him, giving herself a chance to catch the moment in her mind. A decade ago, when she was taken from him, they'd both given up on their dreams of building a future together, yet here they were.

She set her hand on his chest. She'd had her nails manicured with a pale pink gel and white tips just for the occasion. He reached up and wrapped his hands around hers. So warm.

"Can you believe we're actually doing this?" she asked.

He shook his head. "When Ace let it slip that you were still alive, I was shocked." He kissed her palm. "And then all the anger, the hope, the fear that followed—all of it was crippling." He touched her cheek as he stared into her eyes. "You're as beautiful now as you were when they took you from me. It's humbling getting a second chance. Most people don't after a loss like we suffered."

He leaned down to kiss her. She had to find a way to quit looking at all that had been stolen from them

—all those empty years. She saw the same struggle in his eyes and forced a smile.

"This will be a good day," he said. "We can have lunch while we're in Boulder. A whole day, just you and me."

She nodded. "Ivy and Mandy volunteered to help Wynn with the boys, so we don't have to hurry home."

Owen stepped back and set his hand on her door. "Then maybe we'll do dinner out somewhere too."

"Like regular people do."

"Yeah." He chuckled. "Like that."

ADDY HADN'T SPENT much time at all out in the public in the ten years since her abduction. There'd been social events—at her home and others—but she'd tried to avoid as much as she could of them; they were never pleasant experiences.

It gave her no small anxiety being out in the wide open, walking in the winter sun, people all around them. Passersby checked Owen out, even though they were holding hands. Addy couldn't blame them—he was a gorgeous man, tall and hard to miss with his blond hair and pale eyes. She was just glad they weren't staring at her.

When they reached the jewelry store, Owen held the door for her. One of the salespeople came forward to greet them. Owen told her they had an appointment with the store manager. They were taken to an office in the back. It had no windows to let the sunshine in, so the room was only dimly lit by a single desk lamp.

It wasn't a large space, but it was filled with a life-time of collected treasures. Glass barrister shelves lined one wall and were filled with large rock and crystal specimens, art glass, and cloisonné dishes. An old Persian carpet covered the floor. Two club chairs sat before an antique library table. Framed photos around the room showed celebrities who'd apparently purchased their jewelry from this store, all of them featuring a happy man, slightly short and a little rotund. In the older pictures, his hair was black, but in more recent ones with celebrities Addy recognized, his hair was salt and pepper. The room itself had a distinct scent of unsmoked tobacco and sandalwood. On the desk were various tools of a jeweler's trade: loops, microscopes, ring sizers.

Addy folded her arms and sent Owen a glance. He gave her a reassuring smile. "This store and its employees and owner were fully vetted. You're safe here."

"It's like another world."

Owen nodded. "Not what I was expecting."

She took his hands. "I hope I can find what I'm looking for here."

"If not, we'll try someplace else. If we have to use temporary rings for the ceremony, that's what we'll do. I don't want you to settle for anything less than exactly the right ring." He smiled at her.

She was so in love with him—it sometimes just stole her breath.

The storeowner joined them then. He was as jolly as he seemed in his photos. He congratulated them on their engagement, then spent the next half-hour telling them stories from the celebrity engagements he'd been part of.

"Now, Ms. Jacobs, I understand you've come to see our selection of aquamarine and diamond engagement rings."

A staff member brought in two black velvet trays and set them on his desk.

"Why don't we have a seat and design your perfect ring?" the owner said.

Addy exchanged excited glances with Owen, then took the seat he held for her at the owner's desk.

TWO DAYS LATER, Addy was in the kitchen decorating a cake Russ had made for Jim's birthday. He'd made two, actually. A big sheet cake, which she'd already decorated, and a personal-sized layer cake that was just for Jim.

Addy looked up as Augie came into the kitchen. She smiled at him. He gave her the same odd look that he'd often had since his return, like his skin didn't quite fit him anymore.

"What are you doing?" he asked, sitting on a stool. He propped himself up on his elbows to look over the counter.

"I'm decorating Jim's birthday cake. Chocolate cake with chocolate frosting. We have vanilla and chocolate ice cream to go with it."

He sat back and looked at her. "You used to do that for us. I forgot about that."

Addy kept her face relaxed despite his stricken expression. "I did. Even when you were gone, Troy and I would have a birthday party for you. I didn't want him to forget you."

"What happened after I left that day, Mom? Cecil hit you so hard. When they told me you were dead, I believed them."

She nodded. This conversation had been a long time coming. She'd wanted to have it so many times, but always hesitated to start it—she didn't want to further traumatize him by dragging him back into that awful place.

"I spent some time in the hospital. And not long after that, your grandfather and Uncle Wendell realized how bad things were. They helped me get a divorce. They also started looking for you."

"Is it true that Owen's my real dad?"

"It is."

"Is he Troy's dad too?"

"He is now."

Augie nodded. "Okay."

Addy looked at the cake she was icing, glad Augie

hadn't asked for more details. She used the spatula to smooth already-smoothed frosting. "What happened after they took you that day?"

Augie looked away. She saw his gaze bounce around the room and feared he was not going to answer. She braced herself.

"They took me to jail."

"Jail?"

"Yeah. There were bars. I was the only one there at night. It was scary. They told me you were dead, you and Troy. They said if I tried to run away, they'd kill me too. They showed me clothes from you and Troy with bullet holes in them—and a lot of blood. I tried to get away anyhow. I had to know for myself, but I didn't know where I was or where we lived. And there was no one around who could help. After a while, I stopped trying. That's when they took me to live with other boys like me who'd lost their families. I learned to be a cub and live in a pride. Then Cecil came to take me away. He put me with Lion's pride. For a little while. Until he took me from there, too."

Addy stopped what she was doing mid-stroke and looked at her son. "I'm sorry I couldn't stop him from taking you." Her eyes watered. "I was so scared for you."

"I was scared in the beginning, too. But things got better when I went to that first pride. I wonder what happened to them."

"You should talk to Dad about that. We have room here for them, if they can be found."

Augie continued to sit on the stool, leaning over the counter to watch her. Addy was warmed by his presence. Since he'd returned, he'd spent most of his free time with the cubs. But little by little, he was finding moments to be with her, and they were slowly reestablishing their connection.

It was a treasure she didn't mean to squander.

"Are you ready for school next week?"

"I guess. We aren't a normal family, are we?"

She gave him a sad smile. "No. And to be honest, other than what I see on TV, I really have no idea what normal is."

"Me either."

Addy started to decorate the cake with yellow rosettes.

"Lion warned us there would be differences between us and others. He said he didn't know what all those differences were, but that we would know them when we met them and that when we did, we were to keep quiet about our side of those differences." He looked at her. "There are a lot of them, Mom."

"I'm not surprised. But you know what? This stuff, these differences, they teach you about what you do and don't like. And when you find things and people and situations that you do like, just do more of them."

Augie was silent a long moment. "Do you like Dad?"

She nodded. "We were kids together. He was a lot older than me, but he would play with me as much as he could. We had the chickenpox together. I've loved him forever. And I couldn't love him without liking him very, very much. So yes, I do."

Addy changed tips on the icing tube. Augie reached for the discarded one to suck the icing out of it.

"So, tell me," Addy said, "how are you getting along with Troy?"

Augie huffed. "Sometimes he bugs me."

"Why?"

"Because he follows me around. Sometimes I just want to be with the cubs. He's not a cub."

"Ah. I realize you never had a choice about being born first. But you were, so you're older than him. You know how you look up to the cubs? Well, that's exactly how he looks up to you."

"He mimics me."

"That's how he learns, by doing what you do. Dad and I are a lot older than he is, so he can't relate to us in the same way he can with you. He's learning from everything you do, just as you learn from everything the cubs do."

"Oh. I'm like a teacher to him. Like Lion."

"Exactly like that."

He shrugged. "Well, I guess I could let him hang around some."

"That would be nice. Dad and I would appreciate that. You're important to us and to him."

Augie got off the stool. He exchanged looks with her then started for the kitchen door, stopping to look back. "I'm glad I'm home, Mom. I can't wait for cake tonight."

Addy smiled. "Me too, honey."

It was a cold afternoon as Owen waited for his family to have their riding lessons. *His family.* That had a wonderful sound to it. Troy was first up and first to finish. He still took naps now and then, so Owen wasn't surprised when he came over and leaned against his leg. He put a hand on the boy's head. It was awful to realize that Augie had been Troy's age when Edwards took him away from Addy.

"Tired?" Owen asked Troy.

"Yeah."

He picked Troy up and went over to one of the benches set under the eaves of the stable, overlooking the corral where the lessons were taking place.

Troy leaned against him, his cheek against Owen's chest. "Warm enough?" Owen asked.

Troy nodded.

Owen locked his arms around Addy's son—his son—and turned his attention to Augie in the corral.

"Will I be as big as you one day, Dad?" Troy asked.

Owen thought about that. "I don't know. I guess you'll be as big as you need to be, which will be big enough."

"Okay."

The next thing Owen heard from Troy was his soft snoring. Addy came over to check on them. She gently brushed Troy's bangs from his face, then leaned over and gave both Owen and her son a kiss.

Owen was still trying to figure out the right way to be a dad, but judging by the happy look on Addy's face, he'd gotten this one right.

OWEN PLOPPED himself down on his big bed by Addy's feet. He smiled at her, and she smiled back. That was the best thing ever—having her there with him, getting to put their boys to bed. He always read Troy a bedtime story, and Augie, for all his standoffish ways, rolled over to watch and listen.

Slow and steady was the only way he'd build trust with either of them—at least, that was what Mandy had said while teaching Augie how to trot and lope. If it worked for kids and horses, maybe it would work for kids and dads.

"Do you think the boys will be all right in school?" Addy asked him.

He sat up and moved over so he could massage her feet. "I think so. They take after you in a lot of ways, and you were pretty social and loved school. It'll be good for them."

"Owen—I've been thinking about something."

"Oh?"

"I want to have more children."

His hands went still. He lowered his gaze to her feet, fighting the terror that comment sent through him. After a minute, Addy sat up and folded her legs under her. He wished he'd been able to hide his reaction from her, but her perceptive eyes saw everything.

"You don't want more children," she said, careful to keep her voice steady.

Owen met her gaze. "It isn't that I don't want more kids. Rather, it's that I want you more than I want more kids. I just got you back. You're only now returning to good health. We're still figuring out what was done to you. We don't have any idea what the nanos in your system might do to a fetus. There's a lot we don't know."

"So let's find out those answers. If the Ratcliffs come back with your dad and Jax, we could have them do some tests to find out if it's safe for me to have another baby."

"It doesn't look as if they'll be coming back right now. But we can still reach out to them for a consult. If there's the slightest chance that we might be endangering you or the baby, then that's that."

"Let's see what they say, and then make a decision. Their answer may not be cut-and-dry like that."

Owen stared into her eyes, trying to read what was behind this need for more children. "I'm happy with the boys we have. If they're all we can have, I'll still feel blessed."

She nodded, but he got what she wasn't saying.

"This means a lot to you."

"It does. I had my life stolen, Owen. You did too. I want to wipe that out and start over, start as we should have all those years ago."

Owen nodded. "I can understand that. But then again, we are who we are and where we are and what we are. We have to be realistic."

She lowered her gaze. The moment stretched into a long silence, then she said, "The doctor who examined me for STDs said I had significant scarring. There's a chance, even if I'm cleared by the Ratcliffs, that I won't be able to conceive, which is probably why I haven't yet. Or maybe the nanos are keeping me from getting pregnant. I don't know."

Owen reached over and caught her hands, desperately needing to touch her. "This is what I mean about accepting ourselves as we are."

"I'm a woman who wants to be a mother again. That's who I am right now, Owen."

He shut his eyes, then met her gaze as he kissed her palms. "Then I'm the man who'll do everything he can to make that happen."

He leaned back, drawing her with him until she was lying on top of him. Her face, as ever, was serious. He wondered when the fear and worry would be gone from her eyes.

*Slow and steady,* he reminded himself—as with her boys, as with everything in the world that mattered at all. He caught her thighs and pulled them open over his legs, grinding himself against her as she leaned forward to kiss him.

"Have you worked out your vows for the ceremony?" he asked.

"Almost. I keep thinking of things to add. Did you lock the door?" she asked.

"Oh, yeah."

She sat up and pulled her tank off. Owen felt himself tighten at the sight of her bared breasts. He buried his face between them, pressing the soft mounds to the sides of his face. He kissed the sides then drew a nipple into his mouth, rolling it around his tongue. She arched her back then gripped his face and bent close to kiss him.

He wrapped his arms around her back and laid her down on the bed. Their gazes locked as he pulled her pajama shorts and lacy underwear down her legs. He looked at her small triangle of hair, anticipating what he was about to do. He buried his face there, his tongue finding her clit. Addy moaned. He could feel her body tensing and slipped two fingers inside her. He moved his other hand up her body, holding her in place as he pleasured her.

Her hands wrapped around his as her release came. When the last throes eased away, he knelt, still between her legs, and removed his own pajama bottoms. Her eyes, which were normally blue, had deepened to the color of her passion—purple. He held himself and stroked her folds with his cock. She leaned up on her elbows to watch him.

"Owen—" she hissed after a moment.

He entered her then settled himself over her body.

Watching her eyes was an aphrodisiac; he could do it the rest of his life and never want for anything else.

He kissed her, long and slow, fighting his own release, wanting to hold off as long as possible. He spread his legs wider as he moved in her, burying his face in her neck. He was close, so close.

Her orgasm was his undoing, driving him to take her harder. He pounded into her until his release broke free in bursts that racked his body.

It took them both a long moment to settle back into normal breathing. He smiled into her eyes as he eased himself from her. "I love you."

She wrapped her arms around his neck. "That makes my life perfect. I love you too."

# 3

———

"**A**re we sure we don't want Val to be our bartender?" Eddie asked as she closed and locked the doors to the game room a few days later. "He's a helluva mixologist."

"No men." Ivy grinned. "We have good and evil plans to make."

"What is it you have in mind?" Addy asked, feeling a passing shot of tension at the mention of an evil party.

"Whatever you want. We can do absolutely anything," Mandy said. "This is the boss's wedding, so we need to really do it up right, though I'm afraid Ivy and I aren't going to be a whole bunch of fun right now."

Ivy blew a bit of hair from her face. "We'll have to have virgin everything." She and Mandy laughed at that, their hands on their big bellies.

"Before we start, everything's set with the kids?" Remi asked.

"Absolutely," Mandy answered. "The guys are on sole parent duty."

"Then the night is ours, ladies," Remi said.

"We could do a couples party," Ace said, "or a bachelorette party, and let the guys do their own bachelor party, or a game night."

"Oh. Right. Well, I don't know," Addy hedged.

"It's your big day. Make some noise," Remi said.

Eddie and Ace went behind the bar and started blending daiquiris, virgins first, which Ace delivered to Ivy and Mandy.

Fiona told Addy about the bachelorette party they had for Ivy and how they kept sending girls out— most of whom failed—with the challenge to kiss Owen.

Addy laughed at that. "But why did they fail?"

"They chickened out," Fee told her.

"But why?"

Fee looked at her as if she was from a different planet. "Owen's scary as hell."

Addy chuckled. "No, he's not."

"It's his eyes. They're piercing," Remi said. "And he hides his emotions, so he's not an easy read."

Eddie came out from behind the bar. "He's the boss—it's his job to be a hardass." She smiled at the group. "And it's ours to help Addy torment him. So what evil thing can we do?"

Addy looked around at the group of women. Some of them were married, but most of them were in the same situation as she was—in a serious relationship heading toward a wedding. All that was, except Selena, who was quietly leaning against the bar, watching them. Addy wished she'd come join them.

"There is one thing," Addy said. She drank a few more sips of the daiquiri, needing liquid courage.

"Name it," Ace said.

Addy worried whether she should say anything at all, but it had been a long time since she had a group of friends she could talk to, and she could use some female advice. "It's embarrassing."

Ace grinned. "All the better."

"Owen is…um…well…too gentle in bed."

Absolute silence met her comment. God, she shouldn't have spoken. Then Mandy and Ivy quietly started laughing.

"Not at all what I expected you to say," Mandy said, still smiling.

"Nothing to laugh at," Ace said. "I had some of that from Val, too. Given what we've been through, I get it. Add in your modifications, too. It kinda makes me like that hardass even more."

"True," Ivy agreed, sobering. "Very true. May I ask if everything's okay in that area for you? You're healthy enough for sex? Your modifications aren't complicating anything?"

Addy looked at Selena, who'd gone with her to the doctor's. "I am. I'm fine in that way. No problems. I just really would like for him to lose himself, you know? I have no idea how to do that. He's the only one I've ever been with that I wanted to be with…and I don't know how to turn him on." Her eyes watered. She blinked to clear them.

Remi, who was sitting next to her, squeezed her hand. "Forget a bachelorette party, ladies. We need to help Addy plan a fuckfest for her man."

Ivy's jaw dropped and her eyes widened.

Fiona laughed and said, "That's perfect!" She clapped her hands. "Let's do it! But how?"

"I know just the thing," Eddie said, surprising them all. "I need to get my computer."

"Wait, don't go," Ace said. "Send Ty for it. Wondering what you need it for will drive him nuts."

"You're so evil," Eddie said, chuckling. She texted Ty.

A few minutes later, he texted back. *I have your computer.*

*Bring it here,* Eddie texted.

*Come to the living room to get it.*

"I'll go," Selena said. "They won't be able to break me down like they could you."

Eddie opened the door for her. "Be strong."


SELENA WENT down the big hall to the main living room. Val, Greer, and Blade were sitting there.

"I told Eden to come get it," Blade said.

"So you did, but you got me."

"What are they up to in there?" Val asked.

"Girl things," Selena answered, putting her hand out for the laptop.

"What kind of girl things?" Blade asked, his eyes narrowed as he intentionally did not surrender the laptop.

"Whatever kind they want."

"Just remember you're one of us," Greer said.

Selena shook her head, smiling. "I have divided loyalties on this, so I'm being Switzerland."

"You know we can see anything Eddie does on her laptop," Greer said with a grin.

"I don't care. But they're working on a surprise for Owen, so don't spoil it for him." She pointed at Greer. "And don't get them in trouble."

Blade handed her Eddie's laptop. "This should be interesting."

Val leaned back against his chair and spread his arms wide. "You know, I'm an expert on girl things. If you need a consult, just shout. I can be trusted not to reveal secrets."

"There are nine of us females back there. I think we've got girl things covered."

Selena went back to the game room and knocked on the door.

Eddie's voice came muffled through the door as she said, "Are you alone?"

Selena shook her head at Eddie's cloak-and-dagger tone. "I've got the goods. Open up."

Eddie cracked the door then opened it, locking it

again after Selena was inside. She took the laptop, then hurried to the coffee table and sat on the floor, navigating to a website. Selena considered warning her that the guys might be watching her, but remembered she was trying to be neutral. Besides, they'd all been warned about their lack of privacy during their on-boarding into the group.

Addy was sitting on the sofa with Fiona, Remi, and Wynn, watching Eddie's screen. Ace stepped away from the group to snap pics, preserving the evening for the wedding photo album she was compiling for Owen and Addy. Her timing was perfect—the looks on everyone's faces were enough to let Selena know the kind of website they were looking at.

"What?" Eddie asked, hearing their gasps. "Look, it took a long time for me to find Ty. These sites got me through that awful dry spell."

*Boom chicka wow wow* music came on. Selena called up the app on her phone that ran the house's security and shut off the cameras to the room. Maybe the guys could see what the girls were viewing, but they didn't also get to see the girls' reactions to their research.

Eddie and everyone seated behind her suddenly leaned over to the right, tilting their heads to the side. Selena could only imagine what they were watching. Fee's face was bright red.

Ace looked at Selena and busted out laughing.

"Did you get that?" Selena asked.

"Oh, I got it. On video."

Addy frowned as she watched whatever was playing on Eddie's computer. "How is that physically possible?"

"Well—" Eddie looked back at her. "Forget it. Let's not get sidetracked. We have to keep to our mission. I'll find a good vid for what you need to do to Owen."

"Here, I'll do it," Remi said, reaching for the laptop.

"You know," Eddie said as she handed off the computer, "Ty had some sex hang-ups we had to work through, with everything that had happened to him here as a kid. It's hard stuff, sometimes. But we found making it fun, laughing a lot takes the stress out of it."

"No. No laughing during the fuckfest," Remi said. "At least, not in the beginning. Owen has to be out of his mind with lust for you."

Addy nibbled her bottom lip. "But how do I do that? Geez, I'm not a novice at this, but I feel like one."

"Maybe it's in what you wear," Eddie said. "Val bought me some lingerie as a gift to Ty—"

Addy's eyes went wide. "He what?"

"Yeah." Eddie shook her head. "Don't ask. But it worked. I think maybe Val knew Ty had some issues and that what I wore—or didn't—was the tool I needed to break through to him."

Remi grinned. "I wish I'd been here to see that whole thing play out."

"Me too," Wynn said. "So let's go shopping." She frowned as she looked at Selena. "The guys won't open her package, will they?"

Selena shook her head. "Address it to me. If they do, they'll die."

Remi pulled up a page of racy lingerie. "Oh, I want one of those!" Mandy said, but then set her hand on her belly as reality hit. "Well, send me that link. When I'm back in shape after this baby, I'll give Rocco one helluva surprise."

They went through pages of options before finding a lace bodysuit with openings for breasts. Leather pasties with long tassels completed the ensemble.

"That's the one," Ivy said. "It's perfect!"

"Pasties? Really?" Addy complained. "How do I wear those?"

"They have tassels. You make the whole thing bounce around when you walk," Ace said, having come around to see what they'd settled on.

"And then you walk like this," Fee said, standing up to do a sexy strut across the room that had all the girls laughing.

"All right," Addy said. "That's just outrageous enough. Order me one. Size eight." She sent Selena an apologetic glance. "I hope this won't be career ending if the guys do open your mail."

Selena gave her a feral grin. "Won't be my career that ends."

Addy laughed. "So how do I do this, then? What are the logistics?"

"I think you should tease him at a dinner," Mandy said. "See if you can get him to break in front of us."

Selena saw the fear that flashed across Addy's face, and wondered—not for the first time—what terrible things Edwards had subjected her to. "I'm not wearing this in front of everyone."

"Of course not! That's not what I meant." Mandy giggled. "That would just be weird. Wear one of your lovely outfits with it on underneath."

Ivy added, "Pay extra attention to Owen. It won't take him long to get the message. Then follow the script of one of those videos we just watched."

"Just let us know which night you're doing it so we can take care of the boys," Wynn said. "We gotcha covered."

SELENA WENT behind the bar when the party started to break up. What an intense evening it had been. Her body was on fire. She was inches away from driving over to Winchester's to find a hookup.

*Don't do it,* a throaty whisper floated through her mind, startling her enough that she dropped a whiskey glass she'd just picked up from the sink.

Bastion.

How did he know her thoughts? How was that possible? Why did he think she would or wouldn't do whatever it was she wanted, simply to please him?

*It isn't a stranger you crave.*

Ignoring him, she continued cleaning up. The door to the game room had been opened and the women were pairing up with their men. Selena wiped the granite counter of the bar. God, she was tired of being alone.

*You aren't alone.*

Still she ignored that voice. In every way that mattered, she was indeed alone. She had no man to turn to, not a single friend that was hers and only hers.

*You have me.*

She squeezed her eyes shut, fighting tears. Yeah, she had Bastion, a figment of her own mind.

*You've seen me, touched me. I am real.*

Ivy commented to Kelan that he was a lucky man. The look he sent Fiona should have incinerated her. He pulled her close and kissed her.

"Yes, I am." His growly answer came long after Ivy had already left. He wrapped an arm around Fee.

"You sure I can't help, Sel?" Fee asked.

"Nope. Got it under control." She forced a smile. "Go show Kelan what you learned tonight."

He frowned. "What did you learn?"

Fee giggled and took his hand, leading him from the room.

*Show me what you learned tonight.*

Selena gritted her teeth. Ignoring Bastion was

41

becoming increasingly difficult. She yearned to cave and give herself over to him. She was desperate enough to do it, too.

She loaded the dishwasher with the dishes the women had brought over to the bar.

*Come upstairs.*

That stole her breath. Was Bastion here?

*I will be with you in the way that I can. I will not leave you alone when you are in need.*

Selena's heart began to beat hard. She swept the room with a glance, looking for something that needed straightening, something—anything—that would let her delay the inevitable, but there was nothing more to do.

She closed her eyes and instantly Bastion was there, his hand on her cheek, his lips hovering near hers. The memory of his seductive scent slipped through her mind.

She crossed the room and switched the lights off as she left. She touched her chest, feeling her heart pounding, hungering for what she knew was coming. It was almost as if her feet were floating—she wasn't very aware of the long trek down the hall and up the backstairs to her room. She stepped inside and locked her door. The lamp on her bedside table switched on by itself. She walked deeper into her room, searching for her secret visitor.

"Bastion? Are you here?" she asked, seeing no one in her room.

*I'm with you.* Heavy arms encircled her. But she

was alone, so it was only the impression of him there, holding her. How could that be? She opened her eyes and looked around her, flooded by a sense of emptiness when she realized this was all in her head. All of it. The crushing sense of aloneness made her want to vomit. She covered her mouth and headed toward her bathroom.

*Stop.*

As if she hit a wall, she was absolutely blocked from moving forward.

*You are not alone.*

A hand under her chin turned her face toward the floor-length mirror that leaned against the wall. He was there, behind her. Nude, though her body blocked her full vision of him.

*You are my woman, and I will not leave you in need. Give yourself to me and I will give myself to you.*

He was gorgeous. Wild. Tall and broad-shouldered. His thick brown hair was in that man-bun he favored. He moved his arm around her waist and nuzzled her neck. Shivers rippled over her skin like an electrical frisson.

She stared at her reflection as she touched his forearm. She could even feel the coarse, dark hair under her palm as she stroked him. But all of that disappeared when she looked down at herself and saw her hand hovering over empty air.

Her gaze cut to his reflection. He closed his eyes as he pressed his face to the side of hers. He was a beautiful man, in the same way that a craggy cliff is beautiful, and he wasn't in any way real.

*I am not beautiful,* he said—to her ears or through her mind, it was all blending now.

*You are to my soul,* she answered. Truth, those words, but how had she found them? Something about Bastion stripped her to her essence.

He covered her eyes with his big hand, blocking her vision. *Don't look too close. You'll see knots of scars and the terrible things I've done that make me me.*

*I have those scars too.*

He kissed her temple. *I know. But yours make you strong.*

She pulled his phantom hand from her face. *Bastion, what are we doing?* She kissed his palm. His skin was warm against her lips. Her body quivered. How she needed him.

*I will give you release.* His hand trailed down her neck, down her chest to the buttons on her shirt. One opened, then the next.

She pulled her eyes from the image of him standing behind her in the mirror and watched as the third button released itself.

It was a cruel reminder that he wasn't really there with her. She jerked herself away from him, backing up to the wall. Her eyes darted around the room, madly searching for him. How was this happening? How could she feel him if he wasn't physically there?

She looked into the mirror, but it was now empty. She covered her eyes and slumped to the floor. What was she doing, indulging in this? Letting this being in to her mind was potentially dangerous. What if he took over? What if he said and did everything he needed to in order to gain control over her?

What if he used her against the team?

She could feel Bastion's soft efforts to reach her, but she blocked him from her mind. She couldn't continue with this. She knew nothing about him.

And there it was, yet another reality-defying thought.

He wasn't anything. He didn't exist. He really was a figment of her imagination. Maybe she never did really see or touch him in the gym after Max's wedding. Kelan and Greer never found evidence of him when they searched the house that night.

But if that was true, how had he turned on her light or unbuttoned her shirt? She hadn't touched those things. How was any of this happening? And why her? Was she the weakest link on the team? Had her loneliness been an open invitation to him?

She fisted her hands and squeezed her head, reminding herself that he wasn't real. None of this was really happening. Someone was slipping her psychedelics. That had to be the answer. But who? The Omnis had used them on both Fee and Addy. Maybe Ace too.

But no Omnis were in the house.

Had she consumed something no one else had? She'd run errands today with Mandy. They'd stopped for lunch at Ivy's diner. Maybe someone there had

45

slipped her something. Maybe there were Omnis all over town.

God, she was so fucking paranoid. But why was she the only one this was happening to? Had to be because she was the weak link.

The Omnis had somehow hacked her.

She was so fucked.

# 4

K it woke when Ivy got out of bed for the third time that night. She had to be exhausted, running to the bathroom all night. He looked at the clock, realizing it was more morning than night, but you'd never know it from how dark it still was. When she got back under the covers, he pulled her close, spooning up against her back.

"You doin' all right, babe?" he asked.

"I am. Didn't mean to wake you."

"No worries. How about I get up with Case and you sleep in?"

"Is it that time?"

"Soon."

She yawned. "I wish I could, but not today. It's Casey's first day back to school." She ran her hand over his, already spread wide on her belly. "I haven't been nearly as sick with this one as I was with Casey."

Kit nuzzled his face against her hair. "I wish I'd been there for you."

She turned to her back and caught his face. "You've been amazing with this one."

"I'm trying."

"Mandy said Rocco was terrified of having a girl."

"I wondered why they hadn't said anything. So they don't know what they're having either?"

"No."

Kit chuckled. "Rocco's a great dad to Zavi. He'll be great no matter what they have."

"I've been thinking that maybe we should find out what we're having."

"You want to?"

"Yeah. Would help us get ready."

"You gonna tell Mandy?"

Ivy laughed. "I'm going to tell everyone." She drew his face close for a kiss, sleepy and gentle. She was already bed-warm again, and he was instantly burning for her.

He sighed.

"What?" she asked.

"Nothing. Go back to sleep."

She rolled to her side, holding his arm around her belly. "You okay no matter what we're having?"

He kept himself from laughing. Not like he could turn that train around, even if he wanted to, which he didn't. "I just want a healthy baby. And a healthy mom for both of our kids." They were both silent for a long moment. "You sleeping?"

"Maybe."

"I'll see Casey off to school."

"No. No, I'm good."

"So what's up with her, anyway?" Kit asked.

"What do you mean?"

"She's been moping around something fierce the last few weeks."

Ivy turned on her back and stared up at him. There wasn't much light in the room, but Kit could make out her face.

"Are you serious?" Ivy asked.

"Yes. I'm serious. Haven't you noticed?"

"She has a crush on Lion and is brokenhearted that he's leaving for school." Ivy gasped, then struggled to sit up. Kit helped her. "Oh, man. Even more reason to see her off today. Lion's also starting to move in to Fiona and Kelan's place today."

"Ivy, Lion's an adult. Case is a kid. What the hell is she thinking?"

"I've already talked to her. Our hormones get so far ahead of our bodies, you know that."

"What does that mean?"

"It means just that. Your daughter is crushing pretty hard. She's convinced he's the one for her."

"Fuck. I thought I already squashed that."

"With Lion, maybe—not that I think for even a second that he had any interest, since she's still a baby. However, you didn't squash it with your daughter. Don't worry. I've had a talk with her. Something may come of her crush in time, but it may not. She figured out Lion would be about my age when she was twenty-one. That hit home. She called me old."

Kit laughed. "I don't feel old. And if I'm not, you aren't. And nothing better fucking happen between them before they're both old, if at all. Maybe I'll have another word with Lion before he leaves."

"Just let it be. He's going off to college. All kinds of new experiences will happen to him and Hawk. Let's not make a big deal about this. We've seen what happens when parents blow things out of proportion." She reached for his hands. "Your daughter is hurting, though."

Kit sighed. "I hate that I can't fix this one. I can't do a damned thing."

"And that, my love, is the terrible wonder of being a parent."

"You know what I said before about not caring if we're having a boy or a girl? Well, I take that back. Boys are a lot easier. Let's have one of those."

THE CUBS WERE LINED up in two rows in front of the house, backpacks filled with the supplies they'd need at school. Each wore clothes from mainstream society, with warm coats, hats, and gloves. They weren't even all matching. Lion checked them over, regretting their time as wild children was over—for him and Hawk as well.

He hated to be leaving them, but these boys were

strong and fearless. They weren't without family—they were brothers to each other. And they had the families here.

They'd toured the school and its grounds last week over the winter holiday, but none of them quite knew what to expect. This week would be full of assessments, then they'd each be placed into the appropriate classes.

Lion knew he had the same catch-up ahead of him. He hoped they were ready for what was coming. Maybe they'd never be ready; maybe they just had to jump in and swim. He'd had that talk with them. He and Hawk had delayed their departure by a couple of days so that he could help the kids transition into their new lives.

Casey came outside, with Troy, Addy, and Owen following behind. Lion knew Kit and Ivy were watching from the windows flanking the front door. Casey had begged them not to come outside. Beetle was already in the lineup. Troy hadn't been to a public school yet. And Casey had had to sit out several months. All of these kids had their own hurdles to overcome—at least they had that to pull them together.

A big school bus pulled onto the property and turned around in front of Blade's house. There were a few other kids onboard, all of whom moved over to look at the house and kids from that side of the bus.

Lion stood near the open doors and nodded at each of the boys as they boarded. Casey was the last to get on the bus. She smiled at him, but her eyes seemed sad. Maybe she felt the end of their old lives, like he did. As soon as she was on the bus, several of her friends screamed her name. Lion stepped away from the bus, watching as her friends hugged her. The bus driver ordered them to settle down.

He waved as the bus pulled away. When he turned around, everyone looked a little stricken. Wynn and Mandy stood there with Zavi. Mandy wrapped an arm around her large belly and said, "I have an overwhelming need to follow them to school and make sure they're okay."

Lion nodded and watched as the bus drove off the property. "I know what you mean."

"Can we follow them?" Addy asked.

"It's hard letting go," Wynn said. "And I've only been caring for them for a few weeks."

Owen wrapped his arm around Addy's shoulders and led her back inside.

"Where's Hawk?" Mandy asked Lion.

"He's getting a few last things together. We're going to take some stuff down to the apartment with Fee. I wanted to be here for the cubs as long as possible. We can use the next few days to get moved in while they're at school. Then Sunday, after the wedding, we'll head out for the week."

Zavi sniffled and wiped his nose on the back of his hand.

Mandy held his shoulder. "What's the matter, sweetheart?"

"Why can't I go with them? Troy did."

Mandy knelt down and took his hands. "We talked about this. You have to get a little bigger. He's a little older than you."

"But the house is too quiet without everyone there." More tears rolled down his cheeks.

"They've only just left. You don't know how quiet it is."

"It was quiet before they ever got here. At least I had Casey before. But now I don't."

Mandy looked up at Wynn and winked. "Well then, I guess we'll have to make some noise." Using his shoulder for leverage, she hoisted herself to her feet. "I love you, Zavi!" she shouted, throwing her hands out wide.

"I love you, Mom!" Zavi answered at the top of his lungs. "I love you too, Miss Wynn!"

Wynn responded, "I love you both! I love this house! I love my job! I love shouting!"

Lion smiled as the women roared their way into the house with Zavi. Hawk came out carrying several bags. Lion met his serious gaze. He looked as tense as the cubs. Maybe they should do some shouting too.

Lion popped the back hatch to his SUV and tossed one of the bags in. Fee's apartment was fully furnished, so they just needed to bring down their personal items.

Lion punched Hawk's arm. "I think it's appropriate to say, 'Chill-out.' We're good. We're moving on to the next thing."

"What if I liked the last thing better?" Hawk asked.

Lion shrugged. "There's plenty of forest to be wild in, and the woods will be waiting for us if this doesn't work out."

"They call to me."

"Yeah, me too. But we owe it to Owen and the team to make a go of this."

Hawk nodded. "I know."

Fiona came out, dragging two suitcases. Kelan followed her with two more. Fee looked happy. Kelan didn't. Lion and Hawk grabbed her stuff and started loading it, rearranging what was already there.

Kelan pulled her close. "Call me when you get there."

"I'll be with Lion and Hawk. I'll be perfectly safe."

"Call me when you get there."

Fee smiled up at him as she slipped her arms around his waist. "I will."

Lion tried not to invade their private moment, but he couldn't seem to look away. Kelan had no problems showing his affection and need for Fee. That was the one part that worried Lion the most about his next step in life: women.

Kelan brushed his thumb over Fee's cheek. "I love you."

"I love you. We'll be back this afternoon."

"I'm glad." He kissed her. Cupping the back of her head in his hand, he leaned his forehead to hers.

"I want you to work hard this semester. Knock that shit out so you can come back to me."

She nodded. "I might take an extra class or two. Maybe, if I take summer classes, I could finish a semester early. Are we calling your parents tonight?"

"Yes."

Fee ran her hands up his chest. "Are you worried about it?"

"No. I'm looking forward to that."

"Me too." She smiled, then caught his face for a kiss. Lion did look away then.

Kelan opened the front passenger door for her. Lion wasn't certain he ever wanted to fall in love if it felt as awful as Kelan looked.

Lion closed the back hatch as Kelan came over to him and Hawk. "She's my heart. Guard her as if she were yours."

Hawk gave him a sympathetic smile. "You know we will."

Kelan bumped fists with him, then gave Lion a hard glare and shook hands. "Keep your eyes open. We're not out of the woods."

But they were, weren't they? Not only out of the woods but way out in the open, exposed to their enemies.

"I will."

FEE LOOKED at Kelan's happy face that evening. She'd

only just gotten home, and dinner would be served soon. They had a narrow window to make the call to his parents.

She was too nervous to smile back at him. He'd said plenty of times how happy his parents would be to welcome her to the family, but this was the first time she would actually talk to them herself. What if she heard in their voices a resistance to her that Kelan never heard? What if they weren't really happy about her and Kelan?

She wrapped her arms around her stomach. "What if—"

"No more what-ifs," Kelan said. "We're already a couple. This is just a formality. They cannot break us apart because we're already united."

"Right. But what if—"

Kelan raised his brows, his thumb hovering over the digits on his phone.

Fee bit her lips. "Fine. Let's just get this over with." She clenched her teeth and winced.

He grinned and shook his head as he dialed his parents. The call was on speaker, so Fee heard it ring. Maybe they wouldn't be home. Maybe—

"Hi, honey."

"Hi, Mom. How's everything going?"

"Great. And you?"

Fee heard the full question his mom didn't speak.

"Super. Is Dad around?"

"He's right here."

"Then put me on speaker. Fiona and I have some news."

"Oh?"

"Hi, son," his dad said.

"Is she there with you?" his mom asked.

"I'm here. Hi." Fee shot Kelan a glance. He grinned at her.

"Hi, sweetheart," his mom said. "I can't wait to meet you. Any woman who captured my son's heart has to be a rare angel."

Fiona laughed nervously. "I'm no angel." God, couldn't she have said something—anything—else?

"Yes, she is," Kelan said. If Fee didn't know better, she'd think he was enjoying her fit of nerves.

"So have you set a date yet?" his dad asked.

"Honey, don't jump ahead. This is their news to tell."

"As a matter of fact, that's what we were calling about. Fiona and I would like to have our wedding sometime this spring. Any dates bad for you?"

"Are you coming home for the wedding, son?" his mom asked.

"No. We're having it here."

"Hold on. Let me check the calendar."

"Mom's checking," his dad said, "but you know it doesn't matter. Anything she has planned, she'll reschedule."

"We're flexible," Fiona said. "She doesn't have to redo anything."

"Not true, hon. She's been asking me every day

when we were going to get this call. She's over the moon."

"Is she?" Fee asked.

"Yup. Kelan doesn't take these things lightly. When he chose you, we knew he'd found the right one."

"But you haven't even met me yet." Fee's eyes were watering.

Kelan hugged her and whispered, "Told you."

"We love our son," his mom said. "And if he loves you, then we do too."

"I'm really looking forward to meeting you both," Fee said.

"I can't wait. My calendar doesn't have anything written in stone——" his mom said as she came back to the phone.

"Told you," his dad interjected.

"I would just like for you two to consider having it here," his mom said. "Everyone would love to witness your wedding, and it just isn't feasible to have them all travel out to you. Just something to think about."

"We'll consider it, Mom. After we pick a date, I'll have Fiona get in touch with you to work everything out."

"Sounds great. Oh, honey, I am so happy for you. I know your brothers will be too. And I finally get to have a daughter!"

"Thanks. I appreciate the warm welcome," Fee said.

"We're here for you kids. Let us know what you decide," Kelan's dad said before ending the call.

When Kelan put his phone down, Fee gave a little scream and jumped into his arms. "I love them. They are so sweet."

He caught her up close and kissed her. "So you're not afraid of them anymore?"

"No. Well, maybe a little. But more excited than scared."

"Good. I'll talk to Kit and see what he thinks about my scheduling a couple of weeks off this spring. Maybe we time it with your spring break. Or we can wait until school's out in May and do it then."

"That might be best. It'll still be spring. That'll give me and your mom plenty of time to do our planning."

"What do you think about going out there for the wedding?"

"I love that idea, but what about everyone here? I don't want them to miss it. With the babies coming, Ivy and Mandy may not be able to travel yet, so Kit and Rocco are probably out."

"That could free up the rest to come—having someone here to man the fort. We can't all go. We'll talk about it. Really, it just depends on how steady everything here is—and that we won't know until much closer to our date."

# 5

Owen came upstairs from the bunker when Greer alerted him that his dad and Jax had just parked out front. He opened the door just before they rang the doorbell. He shook hands with both of them, feeling that invisible wall click into place.

Jim joined them in the foyer, a fresh dishtowel slung over his shoulder. "Nick, Jax, glad you made it."

"Jim. Good seeing you!" Jax gripped his hand then pulled him close to bump shoulders. "I meant to tell you last time that there's a spot on my team if Owen's ever an asshole to you."

"Thanks, but I'm more worried about Russ than Owen." Jim chuckled. "Your rooms are ready. I can take your things up, if you like."

"Sure. Thanks," Nick said as they handed Jim their bags.

Owen shoved his hands in his front jeans pockets

as he faced his dad and friend. He wished—relentlessly—that things had been different with them. Normal, even, if such a thing existed.

It was foolish to spend any energy on that. They had to go from where they were currently, as he'd reminded Addy.

Owen broke the awkward silence. "So. You want some time to settle in?"

"We can do that later," Jax said. "I want to see my sister."

Owen heard someone running toward them down the hallway leading from his and Addy's suite.

"Wendelly! You made it!" Addy gave her brother a big hug. This could have been any of so many homecomings he and Jax had made when they visited the senator's house.

Jax set her down then held her shoulders while he stared into her eyes. "So this is really happening?"

Addy laughed and nodded. "At last." She gave Nick a hug and a kiss on the cheek. "I'm so glad you were both able to make it." She stepped back and slipped her arm around Owen's waist. He set his around her shoulders.

"I'm happy for you both," Nick said. "It's about time that you get to have your own lives and your own joy." He looked around. "Now where are my grandboys? I brought them some gifts."

"At school," Addy said. "They won't be home until later this afternoon. Are you hungry? Can I make you something to eat?"

"No. We're good, sis. Thanks," Jax said.

She gestured toward the living room. "Then come have a seat." She sent Owen a quick look. "Unless you guys need to have a meeting?"

"Nope." Owen smiled at her. "This is your weekend. No business." He looked at his dad and her brother. "Or not much, anyway. We'll meet later."

"Good. Then let's catch up." Addy sat on the sofa. "I hoped you might bring the Ratcliffs back with you."

Jax shook his head. "That didn't work out."

"Oh." Addy sent Owen a disappointed look.

He squeezed her hand, hoping she wouldn't force the issue.

"So what's the plan for the weekend?" Jax asked.

"I can't wait to show you the gym," Addy said. "Everything's set up. The wedding planners completely transformed it. The flowers are being delivered today. Tomorrow we'll have our rehearsal dinner, then the wedding's Saturday."

"Russ is a little ticked off that his kitchen has been overtaken." Owen smiled at Jax. They'd both run missions with Jim and Russ. Picturing them in a domestic setting was still an adjustment, but given they wanted to open their own B&B, this was a great step for them.

"Still has control issues, huh?"

"Big ones," Owen said.

"The repairs to your house are finished, Addy," Jax said.

Addy looked shocked. "You fixed it? Why didn't you tear it down? Or donate it to the local fire department for training?"

"Because it's yours. It's too valuable to trash."

"I will never go there again."

Owen leaned back and drew her close. Everything she'd experienced was still too close to the surface. "You know, Kelan has a shaman he could recommend to clear the place. He brought him here just before Blade's wedding. I don't buy in to all that, but both Blade and Kelan said it felt better here afterwards."

Addy folded her legs against his thigh. Her blue eyes were big as she looked up at him. "Doesn't matter. I'm never going there again. It can rot and crumble for all I care."

Owen nodded. "Then that's how it is. I would never make you do anything you don't want. Tell my dad about the boys and school."

The redirect worked. She told him all the things the boys had shared about their first days at their new school. Owen met Jax's gaze over her head.

He knew that look. Jax had a lot going on. Owen had every intention of discovering exactly what he was up to.

WHEN OWEN STEPPED into the den that afternoon, Nick was sitting in one of the armchairs.

Owen leaned against the edge of Blade's desk and gave him a nod. "Dad."

Nick returned the nod, studying Owen's face.

"Where's Jax?" Owen asked.

"Here somewhere. I told him you and I needed some time." He left his armchair and wandered over to the French doors.

For a long moment, Nick didn't say anything. Owen would have broken the silence if he'd known how. But where did you start when there was so much ground to cover and you didn't want a single moment missed?

"Where do we begin?" Nick asked, still facing the patio doors.

"I guess it doesn't matter, as long as we begin— and as long as we each get our questions answered."

His dad turned around. They both had the same pale blue eyes. It was like looking in a mirror. Really, Nick seemed more like a slightly older brother than a progenitor. Owen had grown to adulthood without the benefit of his presence or influence, and didn't know where he stood or what they really were to each other now.

"You and Jax left so soon after Thanksgiving—we never had the chance to talk," Owen said.

"We had to get the Ratcliffs to safety."

"They were safe here."

"No, they weren't. Not even then, before Bastion had come prowling around."

"What do you know that I don't?"

"A lot."

"Did you know Jason was the monster he turned out to be?"

"Not at first. Not before you'd already left his household."

"And yet you told me to keep Val safe."

"I knew there was discord between Jason and his son, but in the bigger picture, I thought I was putting you out of reach of the Omnis. Jason had never been involved in the training I'd undergone."

"You never meant to see me again, did you?" Owen asked.

Nick shoved his hands in his pockets and leaned a shoulder against the patio doors. "I honestly didn't expect to live. And then years passed. I thought it was too late to reconnect with you. I did what I could for you behind the scenes—getting you into West Point, getting you into the Red Team."

"Were you involved with setting up the Red Team with Henry and Senator Jacobs?"

"No. I surfaced about the time they were hatching that plan, intent on helping make it happen. I thought they'd returned to our original charter of fighting the Omnis, but then I learned that they were recruiting sons from the families of resistance members. I had a bad feeling they were gathering their enemies into a single, known spot so they could take them out, and realized I'd gotten you deeper in by advocating for your acceptance into the team."

"Did you know Jacobs had been flipped by the Omnis and Henry's allegiances were suspect?"

"Eventually, I did. I also realized that by sending the Red Team overseas to deal with threats that may or may not have been connected to the Omnis, Jacobs had effectively redirected the men who were the most capable of fighting the Omnis here in the U.S. I kept working the channels I had to bring you guys back here."

"But the Army can't operate against its own citizens."

"No, but it can run intelligence ops against foreign agents here in the U.S. Enemy infiltration was the original charter of the Red Team."

"You'll forgive me for doubting your claims to innocence. You were part of the original crew, all of whom went bad—except, apparently, you."

"Believe what you will—"

"I will," Owen interrupted.

"I did what I thought was in your best interests and those of thousands of other innocent people."

"By sending me to be raised by the worst of the Omni officers."

"I didn't know what he was when I gave you to him. No one did."

"Tell me, did he know you were still alive?"

"Yes."

"And did Jacobs?"

"Yes."

"I suppose Henry did too."

"He did, but Henry wasn't bad. He realized Jason was a monster earlier than Jacobs and I did. He started infiltrating the tunnels, learning about the Omnis from the inside out. He tried to counter the oppression by organizing the servants living in the tunnels. When they took his granddaughter, he entered the tunnels full-time, faking his own death so he could protect her."

"He was there when Ace was taken."

Nick's lips thinned. "Perhaps that's why she's still alive."

Owen didn't say anything. Time would surface the truth about Nick.

"I feel as if I've ruined your life," Nick said.

Owen gave him a cold smile. "Let me alleviate that concern: you have to be part of someone's life in order to have a shot at ruining it. As far as I care, you're someone I'm cautiously interested in having as an ally. I don't trust you. I may never trust you. You knew about Addy. You knew about Ace." Owen shrugged. "You could have come forward at any point for any reason, but you didn't. You took the coward's road, hiding instead of facing the choices you made. What I don't understand is why come forward now? Is it because we vanquished your enemies?"

"They aren't vanquished. Not by any means. You've only scraped off the dead weight. What lies beneath is stronger than ever and no longer has the burden of power-hungry leaders to choke them out.

You think you've contained the threat, but all you did was pull out the weeds."

OWEN WAS JUST FINISHING his nightly walk around Blade's house, as had been his habit after Bastion's visits began. Jax had set up a phone conference with the Ratcliffs for the morning. Afterward, work would have to be put aside so he could focus on the wedding. He wanted to spend every minute with Addy that he could; it had been a long time since he'd seen her so happy and excited.

When he circled back to the patio behind the house, Jax was standing there, alone. It was cold outside. Owen was surprised to see him there.

"Something on your mind?" Owen asked as he paused next to his one-time best friend.

"Yeah. Everything." Jax looked at Owen, then back at the shadowy trees at the edge of the lower lawn. "You ready for your wedding?"

"I am. I've been ready for ten years. I'm angry it took so long, and I'm thrilled it's actually happening."

"You have to let go of the bad and embrace the good."

"I'm not quite there yet. Like I'm still pissed at you. And my dad."

Jax met Owen's angry eyes—he didn't say anything, but Owen took it as an opportunity to unload. "Why the fuck didn't you come to me? After all we'd been through?"

"I let myself get used."

"That's it. That's all you got?"

"Yup. I believed the wrong people and spent a long time clawing my way back to the truth. I hurt you. I hurt Addy. The boys. When I figured it out, I shut down the parts of it that I could, as I could. I ordered Holbrook's death, ending the abuse on the cubs. I got you out here to discover the testing happening via the Friendship tithes. I got Hope into the White Kingdom Brotherhood to find Lion." He shrugged. "Those were small victories, but they don't make up for what I didn't do."

"Or what we could have done, if we'd stayed working together."

"Yeah. It's why I brought Nick back to you. Same deal with him. We need you and you need us. This fight's a long way from over. And I'm afraid the worst part is yet to come. The top layer we just cut down was merely a veneer covering what's really happening inside the Omnis."

"The Ratcliffs told us these human modifications have the potential to shift the global balance of power, at best, and could be a human extinction event, at worst."

Jax nodded. "Glad they didn't sugarcoat anything."

"Okay," Owen said after a long silence. He held out his hand. "I'm putting my trust in you." Jax took his hand. Owen's grip turned painful. "I don't trust lightly anymore."

"Good. Now quit fucking breaking my hand. I need it to walk Addy down the aisle."

Owen released him. "Sorry."

Jax shook his hand out. "No, you aren't. You just got to it before I did."

They both laughed at that.

"You know the Legion's not going to leave you alone," Jax said. "Not now that they've found you."

"I know." They stood in the cold, staring into the distant woods. "Addy wants more kids."

Jax looked at him. "You think that's a good idea, after everything she's been through?"

"That's why she was hoping the Ratcliffs were coming back with you. She wanted to consult with them."

"We can talk to them about that tomorrow—unless that's something for a private call?"

Owen gave that some thought. They were all facing the possibility of undergoing the modifications. His team was young and would likely want kids sooner or later. They needed to know how all of this could affect them or their women.

"I guess having the team there is a good idea. It could be an issue for them at some point in the future."

"Right. You sure you have time for a meeting tomorrow?"

"We'll make time," Owen said. "See you in the morning."

Selena was exhausted. In the weeks since Max and Hope's wedding, she'd been walking a thin line between belief in herself and pure paranoia.

The stress was taking a bite out of her.

She had thought, for a short while, that she'd banished Bastion from her mind. She refused to think of him. And since no further anomalies had shown up on the cameras around Blade's, she'd begun to hope that whatever that experience with him had been, it really was nothing more than her imagination.

Until the night the girls planned Addy's fuckfest, when he had come into her room and held her in his invisible arms.

Since that night, sleep had been elusive. She'd thought about taking over-the-counter sleep meds, but she couldn't risk being incapacitated if he tried to take her over again.

What little sleep her weary mind found was shallow. Every time she woke to change positions, she'd wake fully, checking her room, checking her phone for security alerts, which was stupid. Greer had written some code to send alerts when the cameras were mucked with. No point checking her phone if the alerts weren't sounding.

But Bastion didn't need to physically prowl

around anymore, did he? Not when he could use her mind as he wished.

He'd been absent now for weeks. The wait for his next appearance felt like a timer that was slowly ticking down to zero. He was coming soon. She could feel that.

When she woke next, it was still dark outside. She quickly took inventory of her senses and surroundings. All was quiet, but she wasn't alone. She opened her eyes. Bastion was there next to her, sitting up against her headboard. Fully clothed, his legs crossed at his ankles, his feet bare.

She scrambled out of bed, instantly alert.

"You are extraordinarily stubborn," he said.

Selena's gaze darted around the room. She grabbed her phone, checking first for alerts, though none had gone off. Before she could text someone for help, her phone went haywire. Apps flickered on and off, sliding sideways across the screen, and then it went dead. She reached for her panic alert necklace, but it wasn't around her neck.

She tossed her phone to the ground and pressed the heels of her wrists against her temples. What to do? What to do? If she walked out of here—if he even let her—to go alert the guys, what would he do to them?

She lowered her hands. She needed her gun. She could pretend to be reaching for the light and grab her pistol at the same time.

The light came on before she even took a step.

"Go ahead, shoot your bed." Bastion disappeared then reappeared in the same place. "I'm not here, so you won't be shooting me."

Fuck. Selena rubbed her forehead. "I asked you to leave me alone."

"I tried. It would seem I have a weakness I did not anticipate."

"Oh? What would that be?"

"You. Come back to bed. We need to talk. I don't like it when you block me from your mind."

"Too bad. My mind, my rules."

"I would honor that were so much not at stake."

"Where are you? I mean the physical you." God, did that sound crazy.

"I am not far. Just a few hours away." He gestured to the half of the bed he wasn't occupying. "Please, let us talk. I will not touch you."

"Get out of my bed first."

He disappeared, then reappeared standing next to her. "Is this better?"

Selena's eyes moved up his chest, wide neck, and hard, bearded jaw, to dark eyes that were so enthralling she couldn't look away. She caught a faint hint of his scent, more memory than anything else. Of course he smelled delicious. He was a figment of her imagination—why would she create an illusion with an unpleasant odor?

Bastion laughed. "It is my own scent you are enjoying. My pheromones trigger a chemical response in you, as yours do in me. It is distinctive, addictive."

"Except you aren't here, so I can't be smelling you at all."

"You have a clear memory of my scent." He gave her a half-grin. "I wish you could know what you smell like to me. In a sea of a thousand sweet-smelling women, I would find you with my eyes covered and hands bound."

"Just what I wanted. My very own bloodhound."

He laughed again. His teeth were big and white and straight. She couldn't pull her eyes from his smile. He gestured again toward her bed. "Please. I have said I won't touch you."

"And you always keep your word."

He sighed. "Not always. I've failed more times than I'd like to admit. I won't fail you, however."

Selena adjusted her pillows then sat on her bed. When she looked up, Bastion wasn't where she left him.

"I'm here." He was now sitting on her dresser, across from the foot of her bed.

"So, since we're having this awesome convo, let's start with your real name," Selena said, figuring she might as well glean some actionable info from him that the team could use.

"I've had many names over many years. I shed them like a snake sheds his skin, having grown out of what he was. So call me what I am. I am the walls that protect you. I am your fortress. I am your Bastion."

"I don't need protecting."

"You do, but you don't know it yet. All of you here need protection."

"Someone purporting to be my *bastion* would not harm those I love."

"Have I harmed your team? I could have, at any point, eliminated them, killed them gently in their sleep, leaving their women to wake next to dead partners. They are as defenseless as infants to me. Your men are not my enemies, that much I've learned."

"So what do you want?"

"The Ratcliffs."

Selena shrugged. "I don't know where they are."

"Find out and tell me."

"So you can kill them?"

"No."

"Why, then?"

He flickered out. *Bastion! Damn you. I will not let you use me.*

SELENA TOOK the elevator down to the bunker. It was early, but she was hoping to find Greer on duty already. She crossed through the weapons room to ops. Max looked up and smiled, but his expression quickly faded.

He got up and shut the door to the hallway. "Jesus. What's goin' on, Sel?"

Selena met his look a little defensively. "Um. Glad you're back."

He waved that off. "You look like hell."

"Great. Just what every woman wants to hear."

"You aren't a woman; you're a fighter."

"No." Selena glared at him. "No, Max. I am a woman."

Max put his hands up and gave her an odd expression. "Right. Got it."

Selena sighed. "I'm having problems with my phone. Can you check it out?"

"What's it doing?" He took it from her.

She lifted a shoulder. "Just started acting funny. A whole bunch of apps flickered, then it shut down."

Max frowned down at her phone. "Yeah. It's outta juice. Helps if you plug it in now and then." He handed it back to her.

"Huh. Thought I'd just charged it."

"Sel, talk to me. What's goin' on?"

"Nothing. I'm fine. Have a good honeymoon?"

"Best ever."

"Great." She stormed out of the room.

Max was solid. Real. Unafraid.

All the things she used to be.

## 6

Owen's father and Jax joined them in the basement. They made small talk for a little while, waiting for Selena, the last of the team to join them. Greer had called her, but no answer. Perhaps she was suffering from her migraines again, which made Owen edgy; she'd first gotten sick with them when Bastion had been near over the holidays.

Perhaps their infiltrator knew Jax and Nick were with them again and was coming back around. He looked at his watch. If Selena didn't make an appearance in the next few minutes, he'd have Kit send Ace up to check on her. He didn't have a lot of time to waste; his and Addy's wedding was tomorrow afternoon. He couldn't stay in work mode very long. He wanted Jax and Nick to update the team while they were here. Better to get started.

"I asked my dad and Jax to join us today to share

the information they have about Bastion," Owen said to the group. "As I understand it, what's known about him came to the Ratcliffs from peers who visited the researchers running the study Bastion was involved in. Both their friends and the study's organizers have been killed, so this is all we have at the moment, and it's all we may ever have. The Ratcliffs are using their network of friendlies within the Omni World Order to quietly appeal for more information. No clue if or when more detailed info will be found." He looked at his watch. "We have a call with them shortly, but I thought Nick and Jax could get us started."

"We know that Bastion was recruited for a human modification study," Nick said. "He and all the men in the study had military backgrounds. They were between thirty and forty-five, all from different educational and socioeconomic backgrounds. Different races, religions, and nationalities. All very different on paper, but they weren't selected in a haphazard way."

"They underwent intense psychological and physical examination," Jax said. "It's unclear exactly what experiments were conducted during this study. What we do know is that the newly changed men were sent to serve with a private military contractor in various shit holes where extra security was needed."

"This unit was made up of thirty men," Nick said. "Ten died only months in to the experiment, presumably due to complications from the modifications. Another five died in violent encounters with others in their group. The group became polarized with two factions vying for supremacy and eventually turned on itself. Seems it was of no consequence to the study's organizers what happened to the participants within the group. Life was no holds barred in their world, like a group of gladiators fighting each other and their environment for survival."

"We don't know Bastion's civilian identity," Jax said. "A man who was given the name Liege seemed to get squared away early in the trials. He was one of the first to access the new skills their modifications gave them. He led his corps in their discovery of their specific skills. They made him a leader of their group. He kept them alive and fostered their skill growth."

"When did all this happen?" Kit asked Nick.

"Started a decade ago," Owen said.

"So how old is this Bastion?" Greer asked.

Nick shrugged. "Age isn't the qualifier it once was. It's not a determinant of appearance, mental acuity, or physical skill—the modifications they received made sure of that."

"The Ratcliffs said it's believed that these men are among those whose modifications were used to regen their bodies and rewire their brains," Jax said.

"Meaning?" Owen prompted.

"Meaning they have extraordinary mental capabilities," Nick answered. "We'll be talking to the Ratcliffs shortly, so save your questions for them. We wanted to give a high-level introduction to what we're dealing with."

"It's true these mods were early in the game," Jax

said, "but they were the top of the line. Their creators designed these nano agents to get inside their hosts, do their function, and exit, leaving their patients improved without a continuing need for refreshing the nanos."

"And now they've sought us out. Why?" Blade asked.

"My guess? They're after the Ratcliffs," Nick said.

"It's time," Greer said. He dialed the Ratcliffs. The phone speakers were on conference mode, so the whole room heard the phone ringing.

Selena joined them while the phone was ringing. She looked unwell. Shadows were heavy under her red-rimmed eyes. Her skin was paler than usual. She didn't look at anyone when she grabbed a seat at the table. Owen wondered if she was fighting a bug, but she wasn't coughing or sniffling.

Before he could ask if she was feeling well, Nathan Ratcliff picked up the call.

"Nathan—Owen Tremaine here. You're on speaker. I've got my team here, along with Jax and Nick. Thanks for giving us a few minutes."

"Not a problem," Nathan said. "You know we owe you for keeping our girl safe. I've got her mom here with me."

"Morning, Team Tremaine," Joyce Ratcliff said.

"There are two things I wanted to cover today," Owen said. "The first is about Bastion. I know Jax and Nick have talked to you about him."

The phone was silent a long moment. "Be very

80

careful with him," Joyce said. "We try to document as much as we can about every changed human we discover. But we lost track of him and his study peers."

"Do you know what was done to them?" Owen asked.

"Not entirely. Jax asked us to find and secure the research surrounding their trials," Joyce said. "We haven't yet been successful. We are familiar with the team that was running it, however."

"And?"

"It wasn't just superior warriors they were trying to craft. They wanted a psychological Red Team, a force they could use to infiltrate anything—other armies, corporations, research labs, you name it."

"How would they do something like that?" Owen asked.

"They thought they could use their specially encoded nanotechnology to rewire the brain's neural circuits, allowing it perform with extreme efficiency," Joyce said. "It sounds supernatural, but it's not. We've all heard of people who have prescient knowledge of one form or another—someone who knows who's on the other end of a call before ever looking at their phone. Someone who appears to be able to read someone else's mind. Someone who summons a friend just through their thoughts. Someone who knows when someone else is thinking about them. Mediums who can see through others' eyes, who connect with someone, alive or dead, just from touching something that belonged to them. The list of psychic skills is endless. Those come from neural networks that are or aren't active in any of us. These are natural skills that lie dormant in most of us. The researchers working on Liege's group isolated certain neural networks and developed nanos to activate them."

"Can you be more specific about what enhanced skills we're dealing with from Bastion and Liege's men?" Blade asked.

Selena coughed and lurched to her feet. Once there, she seemed lost for a moment, her eyes shooting around the room. She went over to a sideboard to pour herself a cup of coffee.

"Friends of ours were able to visit with the study's organizers during the active years of their research," Joyce said. "They were allowed to take notes, but weren't given much detailed information. We have their notes—I am making some assumptions and may be overstating things, but it's my understanding that Bastion and his group may have developed extreme psychic skills."

"Such as?" Owen prompted.

"They might be able to access minds that are open to them. They could potentially induce hypnosis —even over long distances—or impose trance states. They could have the ability to manipulate physical things via telekinesis. They could alter energy around them, interrupting electrical currents—in humans and things. The notes from our friends suggest these abilities developed differently in different participants. Beyond purely psychic abilities, they have enhanced physical abilities. Superior strength, endurance, senses, cognition, memory, motor skills."

"They're perfect." Selena's voice was quiet, but the whole room heard her. "There's no way we can effectively fight them." She sipped her coffee.

Owen looked at his dad. "Not yet. But we may, soon." His dad, and the training he was about to start could be their key.

"Can these enhancements be reversed?" Kit asked.

"That depends on several factors," Nathan said, "like how long the person has existed in an altered state—or rather, how established their altered state is, how old he or she was when they were altered, their general health, etc. In most cases, reversing these modifications means killing the changed person. If their modifications are dependent on a consistent supply of nanos, then weaning them from those nanos might be possible, but won't be a quick fix. Going cold turkey on their supply would absolutely kill them— and probably within months, if not weeks. Their bodies have adapted to performing at certain levels, and when that is suddenly no longer possible, their systems rapidly fail. For those whose enhancements have been overtaken by their biology—no, the changes can't be reversed because they're being naturally regulated by their bodies."

"But these beings can be killed," Greer said.

"Yes. Of course," Joyce said. "But killing them becomes exponentially more difficult, depending on their skills and their proficiency in using them. And because they heal rapidly, anything less than a catastrophic hit probably won't end them."

"I fought some of these enhanced guys at Wynn's house," Angel said. "Felt like they were hopped up on steroids, but they weren't invincible."

"Those were some of the Omnis' newly minted fighters. They hadn't undergone their training yet," Nathan said.

"I have a question for you, Owen," Joyce said. "I understand Bastion has been visiting your head-quarters."

"That's true." Owen exchanged glances with Selena. She looked tense.

"Has he connected with anyone in particular?"

"He's affected several of us in different ways. He spoke to my son," Owen said. Selena looked brittle enough to break. He wished he didn't have to say what knew he had to. "He also has taken an interest in one of my team members."

Silence on the other end of the line, then Nathan asked, "Which one?"

"Me," Selena said, holding her hot mug in both hands. "He's stalking me."

"Selena, right?" Joyce asked.

"Yeah."

Joyce sighed. "Our friends discovered, during their

visit, that there was an unintended side effect of these enhancements."

"And that is?" Owen asked.

"There are hormonal changes that occur because of their altered biology," Joyce said, "which, when combined with their strengthened intuition and enhanced senses, means intimate relationships with anyone not perfectly compatible with them are less than pleasurable to the changed person. Theories why this is include the possibility that they are able to qualify a potential mate's capability to successfully reproduce. The biologics of their changed bodies produce significant incompatibilities with most potential sex partners. The ones with mutations are effectively sterile when breeding with unchanged humans."

"Except for someone who is resonant with them," Nathan finished for her.

Selena looked shocked. "So you're saying Bastion finds me 'resonant' with him? I have no choice in this?"

"We're saying he may have come looking for us, but he's returning because of you," Joyce said.

"What can I do about it?" Selena set her mug down.

"Without extreme training, nothing," Nathan said.

"I can leave."

"He'll find you again. He knows your energy signature. Like a bloodhound searching hundreds of miles for a lost child, he will find your scent and find you, even if your 'scent' is just an electrical current. He's wired in to you."

"Bloodhound, huh?" Selena sent a panicked glance around the room. She looked like she was starting to hyperventilate, then stomped out of the bunker.

"What can we do?" Owen asked the Ratcliffs.

"Get her out of there," Joyce said. "Get her someplace unfamiliar to her. Don't talk about it in front of her. Consider that he's with her at all times now."

Fuck. Owen met Jax's hard eyes. His friend had offered safe harbor earlier. Maybe he'd send Selena with him. She couldn't be alone—she wouldn't be safe.

But then, nor would any of them while she was with them.

Jax read him clearly and nodded.

"What was the other topic you wanted to talk about?" Joyce asked. "You said there were two things…"

"I'm marrying Addy this weekend," Owen said.

"We know," Nathan said. "We're happy for you and sorry we aren't able to be there with you."

Owen nodded. He looked at his team. "As you know, the Omnis did some experimenting on her."

"Right. How's she feeling?" Joyce asked.

"She's fine. Stronger every day." Owen sighed. "This is something of a personal topic, but given the situation these enhancements are causing, I don't think it's inappropriate to bring it up here. Addy would like more children, but we don't know if that's possible, given her situation. In light of what you revealed here, is it possible that her biological changes are incompatible with me?"

"Yes," Joyce said. "It is quite likely. There are many factors at play. We would need to examine both of you before being able to give an accurate answer."

"Then perhaps that's something we can schedule after the wedding."

"Anytime. Our schedules are open."

## 7

K it's phone rang as soon as they hung up from the Ratcliffs. Conversation stopped as he took the call. "Sel—" Pause. His shoulders dropped. "You can't do that." He shook his head. "Let's talk this over—" The call must have ended, because he lowered his phone and stared at it.

"Another migraine?" Owen asked.

Kit looked shocked. "She just quit."

"Shit." Owen started for the hallway between the conference room and ops.

Ace hurried after him. "I'm coming, too." In the elevator, she looked at Owen and said, "Selena and I had a pact."

He hit the up button. "What kind of pact?"

"That I would be there for her if she lost her shit."

Owen faced forward and ground his teeth, almost afraid of what he'd find in Selena's room. They took the backstairs up to her room. He knocked on her door.

No answer.

"Selena, we need to talk," Owen called through the door.

"It's not locked."

Owen went in first. Selena was bent over a pile of clothes, shoving things into a duffel bag. She flashed a glance at him and Ace. Owen saw faint bruises on her temple beside her eyes—something he hadn't noticed in the weaker light of the bunker.

He leaned against her dresser, next to a column of empty, opened drawers. Ace moved about the room. Owen suspected she was checking for a man neither of them could see.

"Talk to me," Owen said, folding his arms.

"I'm leaving. I'm done," Selena said.

"Where are you going?"

Selena straightened. She looked at him then at the wall behind him, no ready answer coming to mind.

"This is because of Bastion, isn't it?" Ace asked.

Selena glared at her.

"Is he here?" Owen asked. Greer had a protocol in place to alert them. Nothing had been triggered, yet Selena looked spooked as hell.

She resumed packing. "He's not here. He's some-where three hours or so from here."

"How do you know?" Owen asked.

"He told me." Selena stared at her open duffel bag. "He was here, this morning." She shook her head. "Not exactly here, but"—she waved her hands around the room—"here."

Owen felt the sharp edges of a headache beginning. He wondered if he was just picking up on Selena's raw energy. He walked over to her, intending to stop her from packing, but the pain in his head spiked. Was this what Selena had been experiencing? He felt nauseated.

Selena saw him stop without coming nearer. She shook her head. Her eyes watered. She backed away from him, holding a hand out. "Get away from me."

Owen stood his ground, wincing from the pain blazing in his brain. "Selena, you have to stop. You're not going anywhere."

"No." She shook her head. "I mean get back. Go back over there." She pointed to where he'd just been leaning against her dresser.

He did back up a step, and another, and as he did so, the pain in his head eased—more with each step. "What the hell's going on?"

"It's Bastion. He's doing that."

"So he is here." Owen looked around the room. Ace shook her head at him.

"No. He's not in here." Selena waved her arms around again, indicating the space of her room, then poked at her head. "He's in here."

Owen remembered Jax saying Bastion and his crew had telepathic, telekinetic abilities. Stuff that existed only in far-fetched fiction.

Selena covered her mouth with her hand, fighting

back a ragged sob. "I have to go. He can get to us through me. He doesn't have to be here to attack us."

The pain in Owen's head was only a dull throb now. "You're saying he caused the pain I just felt?"

"Yes."

"Why?"

Selena sent Ace an embarrassed glance. "Because you and I— Because I had feelings for you once. Sort of."

"Is he hurting you?" Owen's eyes narrowed.

Selena shook her head then gave Owen a terrified look. "How do I know that he's real? What if this is some psychedelic-induced craze? Or a full-on mental breakdown? How do I know?"

"*I* know." Owen gave her a resolute look. "You aren't crazy."

"And Bastion's real," Ace said. "We just had a debrief on him."

"You aren't off the team, Sel," Owen said.

"My being here endangers all of you," Selena said. "I have to go."

Owen sighed. "Maybe that is best. For now. Finish packing. I'm going to send you someplace safe."

"Where?"

"Away from us. I can't tell you specifics. Just know that it's only until this blows over—or until we know how to deal with him. You'll leave after the wedding."

"I should go now."

"I don't have arrangements made yet." Owen started to leave, but paused. "Please avoid the bunker for now, but other than that, there are no restrictions on your movements in the house. You aren't going to reveal anything Bastion hasn't already seen. Don't leave the property."

Ace confronted him in the hallway. "She's not going alone."

Owen was heading toward the backstairs, forcing Ace to keep pace with him. "She won't be alone."

"I'm going with her. I told her I had her back."

Owen sent Ace a glare. "We all have each other's back. You're staying here."

Ace stopped walking. Owen stopped too. She gave him a wounded look, then pivoted and went back to Selena's room.

He couldn't tell her why. He didn't know if Val had ever told Ace that he and Selena had briefly had a thing—or contemplated having a thing, anyway. It hadn't amounted to much for either Owen or Val, since she wasn't the right one for either of them and none of them felt like playing games. But Bastion had ferreted out Owen's passing interest in Selena; he would discover Val's as well—if he hadn't already.

Owen couldn't risk that situation backfiring. If Ace went with Sel, then Val would go too, and whatever Bastion was, he was capable of causing Val harm —a thing Owen had no doubt the bastard would do.

Owen returned to the conference room in the bunker. Silence settled over the room.

"I have declined Selena's resignation," he told the

group. "Somehow, Bastion's gotten his hooks in deep with her. She fears he may use her against us."

"Not an unfounded fear," Nick said.

"She can't stay here," Owen said.

"I can take her to Addy's house," Jax said.

"I was thinking that."

"I'll get my team back there," Jax offered.

"Good. It won't be forever," Owen said, "only until we can figure out a way to deal with the changed ones, figure out what they want."

"I'll go, too," Nick said.

Owen shook his head. "You're due to start your training. We need that to stay on track because we all need to learn as you do."

"My trainer can come to me there," Nick said.

"When is she going?" Val asked.

"Sunday," Owen replied. "Maybe even Saturday night, after the wedding. He's hurting her. She has to get out of here for her own well-being."

"Ace and I will go with her," Val said.

"No, you won't," Owen nixed that. "She'll have my dad and Jax—and Jax's team. She'll be in good hands."

Val shook his head. "She doesn't know them. At least one of us should be with her while Bastion's attacking her."

"Jax and Nick are only peripherally attached to us. He could use any of you to get back here to us. He doesn't know them. She goes alone with them."

"How do you know he isn't going to step up his

game against her in order to get her back here where he can use her?" Blade asked.

"I don't. She refuses to be here while he's doing this. I'm accommodating her request." Owen looked at Jax. "If her situation worsens, you're to let me know immediately."

Jax nodded. "I will."

"It's possible the trainer I'll be working with will know some options for us, some countermeasures against Bastion she can put to use," Nick said.

Owen nodded. "If not him, then someone the Ratcliffs know may. Find someone we can consult."

"Copy that." Nick slowly smiled.

"What?" Owen snapped.

"Nothing," Nick said, his smile widening. "I'm taking orders from my son. That's fucking weird. And awesome."

Owen shook his head. "Nothing is what we expect it to be."

"That's true," Nick agreed. "None of the old rules, systems, or paradigms apply in this new world. We need to figure it out fast and get onboard or get run over, 'cause this shit is spreading."

OWEN TOOK the elevator back up to the first floor, coming out in the bedroom next to his. Addy was there, in the closet, talking to Mandy and Ivy about her wedding dress. He'd forgotten that she was using that closet to hide her wedding finery.

"Addy?" Owen called, careful not to look into the closet.

"Owen! You can't be here," Addy scolded him.

Owen bit his lip. The last thing he was worried about was some hypothetical curse that his seeing her wedding dress would cause. But she cared, so he cared. "I'm not looking. I need to talk to you."

Mandy laughed and touched his arm as she and Ivy went past. "The room's yours. Addy, we'll be in the living room if you need us."

Addy came out of the closet. "What's wrong?" she asked.

"I need a favor."

"Anything. Of course."

"You remember the scare we had last month when Greer discovered we'd been infiltrated?"

"Yes."

"Well, it seems this person has been 'visiting' Selena —not physically but mentally. Somehow he gets into her mind. She fears he may use her to get to us. We don't know what he's after, but he's compromised her. Would you mind if I sent her to your house for a little while?"

Addy shivered. "It's a horrible place, Owen. Especially in the middle of winter."

He nodded.

"If she's being stalked, isn't it a dangerous place for her to be? It's so remote."

"She won't be alone. Jax and my dad will be with her. Jax is going to reassemble the team that he had there."

"If she'll be safe, then yes. Use it for as long as you like."

"Thank you."

"When are they leaving?"

"After the wedding."

"I'd hoped to have more time with my brother."

Owen nodded. "I know. And I'm sorry. We'll arrange another visit as soon as we can. I spoke to the Ratcliffs a moment ago." He reached for her hands. What he had to say must have been written all over his face, for a shadow passed across her features.

"And?"

"There's some evidence that you and I may not be able to have kids. They need to have some samples from us both to do more analysis. It's possible that I may have to take the modifications in order for us to be compatible."

"That's too dangerous. I almost died."

"There are a lot of different kinds of modifications. They would need to know more about yours before deciding on mine. And it's entirely possible that it's not the issue for us at all. But there will have to be more analysis done before we'll know."

She looked crushed as she nodded, and even though she smiled, the sorrow was in her eyes. "I understand. You know what? I'm over it. We have two beautiful boys. We're very lucky."

Owen nodded. "We are."

"And tomorrow I get to marry my best friend."

"So do I."

"I love you."

Owen pulled her into a tight hug. "Not as much as I love you."

EVERYONE INVOLVED in the wedding ceremony gathered in the hallway outside the doors to the gym. Addy had been in and out of the room as it was being set up for them, but when Blair, the wedding planner, opened the doors for their rehearsal, the full effect hit her.

A huge tent had been set up in the room. Stepping inside it was a clear break from one reality to another, one that was mystical and full of extraordinary possibilities.

The tent glowed from streamers of fairy lights interwoven with pale aquamarine banners that were draped from the peak of the tent. Other lights strategically placed cast an icy-blue hue over the far edges. Garlands of gardenia leaves and flowers highlighted certain areas of the venue. Chairs with pale blue seat covers surrounded tables draped with white tablecloths. The place settings featured large hand-blown glass chargers in the same color as Addy's engagement ring. The lighting and pale blue colors gave the tented space an ice palace effect.

There were areas set up for a bar, dining, and dancing. Two rows of chairs had been arranged on the dance floor where the wedding ceremony would take place.

In front of the chairs was a focal-point arch made from raw wooden branches interwoven with more gardenia garlands and white roses. In front of it was a podium for the ceremony's officiant.

Blair talked them through the organization and flow she'd planned for their event. Addy didn't hear all of it. It wasn't until Owen took her hands and smiled at her that she felt centered again.

"Ready to step through this?" he asked.

"I am." She looked around at the people near her. Owen's dad. Wendell. Her boys. Theirs was a small wedding party. Nick would stand with Owen and Augie. Wendell would walk her down the aisle then stand with her and Troy. She hadn't wanted to select a maid or matron of honor simply because she'd come to love all the women at headquarters equally and hadn't wanted to pick one over another.

At Blair's direction, Owen, Nick, and Augie stood to the right side of the podium. Little Troy practiced his solemn walk down the aisle, carrying the ring pillow, then went to stand to the left of the podium.

Blair directed Wendell to lead Addy last. Of course he wanted to march right through the channel of chairs, but Blair had them start over, moving forward slowly. She gave him a cadence to chant silently to himself.

At the podium, he paused briefly to settle Addy next to Owen. She smiled at Owen, only semi-listening to the next instructions, which were for her to give her bouquet to Wendell.

"I have to hold a bouquet?" Wendell asked.

"Yes, of course," Blair said. "Addy needs her hands free to hold Owen's. And you're standing up for her."

"Could we have a vase nearby that I set it in?" he asked.

"Wendell," Addy said, "don't be silly. You're not less of a man for holding my flowers."

He gave Owen a wink that made him laugh, and Addy realized he was teasing. "Maybe it's not too late to pick a bridesmaid?" Wendell suggested.

"It's quite too late," Blair snapped, not catching his humor.

"Fine. I'm man enough to do this."

Blair went behind the podium. "The ceremony will be organized in these sections. Introduction. Statement of intent. Vows. Ring exchange. Conclusion." She looked at Troy. "Tomorrow, when the man standing here mentions the rings, you'll come forward with them on the pillow. You can practice that now." She watched him step away from Wendell. "That's right. Offer your father the pillow first. He'll take your mom's ring. Then offer your mother the pillow to take your dad's ring. Perfect. When that's done, you return to stand next to Uncle Wendell."

She smiled at Troy. "Very nicely done! Now, when

the ceremony is finished, Owen and Addy, I'd like you to face your friends and give the photographer a moment to snap your picture. After that, my team will remove the chairs here, and you will pose for a few more pictures.

"While that's happening, your friends will have appetizers and libations from the bar. Then we'll lift this back curtain"—she pointed off to the side, where a small platform stood for the band—"and open the dance floor. Shortly thereafter, dinner will be served. Your friends will make toasts in your honor. At the appropriate moment, I will invite Addy and Owen to the empty dance floor to share your first dance as a couple. About a half-hour after that, you will both cut the cake.

"What unfolds the rest of the evening is up to you. My staff will stay and serve you in any way desired. We'll return in the morning to clean up after the party. There is nothing you need to do but attend and give yourselves over to our capable hands. Do you have any questions?"

Addy's mind was buzzing with love and excitement, everything but questions. She shook her head. "We'll follow your lead tomorrow." She looped her arm through her brother's. "And Wendell will not fuss about the bouquet."

Blair pressed her hands together in front of her. "Very well. Then that's all for tonight. My staff and I will be back late in the morning to do the finishing touches. You have my number. If you think of any last-minute things to discuss, don't hesitate to call me."

The small wedding party remained behind a moment after she left. "Blair has to have prior military experience," Nick said with smile. "She runs this thing like a drill sergeant."

"It sounds well organized," Addy said. "It's really such a relief to have her help."

"Dad, Jax, you mind taking the boys in to supper? We'll be along shortly."

"You bet." Nick opened the door to the hallway. "Come along, boys. We'll see what everyone else is up to."

Addy turned to Owen, feeling a little breathless. Tonight was the night to execute the plan she'd hatched with the other women. But she wasn't certain she could go through with it. Everything was already arranged. Troy was having a sleepover with Zavi. Wynn had worked out a sleepover for Augie with the cubs. She and Owen were off the clock tonight.

"What's on your mind?" she asked.

"There's one more thing we need to practice," Owen said.

"What's that?"

"Our first dance."

"If we practice it, then it won't be our first."

"We have no witnesses. No one will know." He took his phone out of his pocket and switched to a playlist they'd settled on for the wedding. He set it as loud as possible, but the little phone speaker still made the music sound tinny. He smiled and held out his left hand. She took it and let him lead her into a formal slow dance. The whole time, she stared into his eyes.

He was, in all ways that mattered, a gentle man and a gentleman. How would he react to what she was about to do to him? Maybe she should do it here, while they were alone.

He smiled at her. "You look like you're about to eat me."

Her gaze lowered to his lips. "I want to."

He arched a brow. "We don't need to go to dinner, you know."

"We do. It's our rehearsal dinner. Everyone will be there." Oh, God. How could she do what she and the girls had planned for tonight?

He drew her into his arms while still dancing with her, his thighs pressing against hers. "Then we can be late."

She wondered if he could feel the pokey tassels of her pasties. She hoped not. That would ruin everything.

"You seem tense." He frowned. "You okay with what's happening?"

"I'm fine."

"Your eyes say otherwise. They're a brilliant purple. Royal purple, in fact."

"I'm just excited."

"I can see that." His smile was very male. "Let's go have dinner, get it over with so I can have you alone to myself."

She nodded. He shut off the music, then led her from the room. Could she do this? Become the wild seductress that would lead him to abandon all his inhibitions?

And how was what she was about to do any different than what Cecil had done to her on so many occasions?

A lot, actually.

He wasn't cuffed to a table, and no one was naked.

## 8

 _____

Addy sat near the head of the table, just to Owen's right. Owen never said much during their suppers, but he watched his team and listened to their banter.

He was so handsome. Didn't matter if he wore a T-shirt or a suit or his tux—he always looked composed and in control.

What would it take to shake that composure?

Addy slipped her foot from the strappy high-heeled sandals she was wearing, then stroked the back of Owen's calf with her toes.

His eyes widened. She couldn't hide her smile when he gave her a disbelieving glare. She couldn't tell if it was a silent warning to stop…or not stop.

She hooked her heel over his ankle and pulled his leg a little closer. He leaned an elbow on the table and leaned close to whisper, "Keep it up. I will carry you out of this room and go straight to our bedroom."

Heat flooded Addy's face. Her lips parted. "You wouldn't dare."

"Watch me."

She bit her bottom lip. He looked as if he were about to scoot his chair back. One of the team asked him something, diverting his attention.

Addy couldn't stop the throaty giggle that came out. She stared at her plate, wondering how close they were to the meal being over. She checked the still-full plates around the table and realized they weren't close at all.

She looked at Owen, who met her gaze. Heat trickled down her spine. She bit her bottom lip. His brows lifted. She reached over with both feet and stroked them down one of his calves.

He slammed his napkin on the table and scooted his chair out. Addy gasped, shocked that he was following through with his warning. He pulled her chair out too, then scooped her up.

"Excuse us, please," he said to the room.

Addy hooked her arms around his neck and buried her face in his neck as she held on to him. Silence met their exit, then male laughter as they made their way down the hall.

"You didn't think I'd do it, did you?" he growled as his long stride moved them into the hallway toward their suite.

"No." She giggled. "I thought you had more fortitude."

He shook his head. "I've got nothing when it

comes to you." He set her on her feet at their door. She leaned against him, loving the feel of his hard body. He caught her face and crushed his mouth to hers. She wrapped her arms around his waist and pulled him closer.

Owen broke the kiss, then tilted his head and took her mouth again. Addy opened for him, offering him everything he wanted. She bent her knee and moved it over the side of his leg. He caught her up by her waist. She spread her legs on either side of his hips and held his face, kissing him as he opened the door to their room.

"We'd better move inside, away from the cameras. Don't feel like pausing long enough to stop them."

She laughed. "Oh! I left my shoes under the table."

"We'll get them later."

"They're part of my outfit."

"What outfit?"

"You'll see." She smiled at his hissed breath.

He cornered her against the wall in the short hallway into their room. "Show me now."

She shook her head. "You don't get to run everything."

"Yes, I do. I'm the boss, remember?"

She pushed him back to the opposite wall. "Not in this." Stepping away, she began to unbutton her black blouse. She'd chosen it to hide what she was wearing underneath. She left her shirt on but open while she unzipped her jeans. She pushed them down her hips, then turned her side to him as she stepped out of them. Cool air covered her mostly bare ass.

"Addy, you're killing me."

She looked at him over her shoulder. His face was like carved granite, his entire focus on the skin she was revealing. She pushed her shirt off her shoulders, dropping it to the ground. His gaze moved up her body.

"Jesus Christ. What are you wearing?"

Addy faced him, showing him the front of the skimpy bodysuit she wore. It was fitted black lace over an open-crotch panty that tied in the back. The bra portion had open cups and a regular bra strap in the back. The ensemble came with sticky pasties that had black tassels. The whole outfit was a shocking departure from her normal sweet but conservative lingerie. Owen's mouth hung open.

He turned from her, but she pushed him back—almost afraid he was going to run from the room. "Did I say you could move?" she asked.

He held his hands up. "I was just going to turn the light on. I want to see all of you."

"I'll get it." She turned her back on him, knowing she was showing him her ass, framed by the bodysuit's straps that were tied at the small of her back.

"What new torture is this, Addy?"

She flipped the light on, then slowly turned around. "One just for you. And me. Do you like it?"

His gaze moved over her body. "Fuck yeah. Come back here."

She leaned against the door and moved her arms up over her head, stretching like a cat. She'd never seduced any man before and really had no idea how it was done. She hoped like hell Owen didn't suddenly laugh at her, because she'd totally lose it.

A quick glance at him, and she realized laughter was the last thing on Owen's mind. He was captivated by her body. Every move she made tightened the tension in his face. The corner of his jaw was clenching. His nostrils were flared.

She wanted to draw this out until he hit a breaking point, but she may have overestimated his endurance. She slowly walked toward him.

"So how's this gonna go, Addy? You running this show?"

"I am. And it goes how I say it goes."

He reached out and let the tassels spill through his fingers. "Uh-huh. I never figured you for cruel. Tell me I'm allowed to touch you."

"You may."

He caught her breasts in his hands. She arched her back. He groaned. He moved his hands around her back and down over her ass. He followed the straps of the bodysuit between her legs; she knew the exact moment he discovered it was an open-crotch outfit. She lifted her leg against his thigh, letting his fingers work her secrets. He stopped just as she was about to come.

She frowned at him. "Now look who's being cruel."

He pulled her against him. "We can end this right now."

"Soon enough." She pushed him back against the wall and started to unbutton his shirt, moving slowly from one button to the other.

He growled and shoved her hands away, managing to free two of his own buttons before she took over again. "My show, not yours."

He laughed and leaned close to kiss her. "Yeah, well, if you don't speed things up, this show's going to end right here right now."

She didn't move any faster as she finished unbuttoning his shirt and then his cuffs. He shrugged out of it, then yanked his tee off before she had a chance to do it. "You're cheating."

"No, only trying to survive."

She had her hands on the belt of his jeans, blocking him from tackling that. She slowly pushed the leather through the buckle and unfastened it. She looked up at him as she opened his jeans. His hips were so lean that, without the belt fastened, his jeans slipped down his hips a bit.

Addy ran her hands up his chest, over his ribs and pecs, arching her body against his, teasing him as he watched the tassels still covering her nipples. He caught her face and kissed her, bending his head to the side to sink his tongue between her teeth. When he pulled back, she slipped her fingers down his hips, between his skin and underwear, pushing everything down to bare his heavy cock.

He had thick thighs and his pants were not loose, so she left them at the top of his thighs as she knelt between his legs. His breathing was shallow. There was no humor in his eyes. In fact, all emotion had been choked out by the desperate hunger burning in his gaze.

Maybe she was doing this right.

She stroked his thighs then moved around to his taut butt. His cock was thick and long, jumping a bit as she touched everywhere but there. She caught it in both hands and brought it to her mouth, letting her tongue just flick over the crown, looking up at him as she licked him. His teeth were bared.

She let him go, then lifted one of his ankles so she could untie his boots.

"Forget my fucking boots," he growled.

"You're not giving orders tonight."

He heaved a sigh and leaned against the wall, letting her have her way. He cupped himself as she removed his boots. She licked her lips, just inches from him, then reached up and pulled his jeans and underwear down his legs.

Owen stepped out of his pants and spread his legs, holding himself for her as she opened her mouth. Her arms went around his thighs, holding his ass.

She licked the sensitive underside of his cock, smiling as she let her tongue trace the edges of its crown. She knew he was close to breaking. How much more could he take?

She opened her mouth and took him in, deep into her throat. He pumped twice in her mouth, then pulled and yanked her to her feet.

He was no longer asking permission for anything. He took her to the bed and pushed her down on it, turning her onto her stomach. He lifted her hips and slid into her, a hot, hard rod. He was holding her ass cheeks, taking his pleasure, slow at first but in seconds, he was slamming himself into her. It felt so delicious. She closed her knees, wanting to feel even more of him, but he leaned over her and opened her thighs back up. With one final hard thrust, he released himself.

It was magnificent. Powerful…but she still hadn't come, and she was so very hungry for him. She whimpered a complaint when he pulled out of her. He didn't give her any time to think about it, though. He rolled her over then knelt over her, lowering himself onto her body.

His beautiful pale blue eyes stared into hers. The color was high in his cheeks but his eyes were somber. His thumbs stroked her face for a moment, then he leaned down and kissed her. Gently, as if they had all the time in the world. As if her body wasn't still on fire. As if there was no need in the world now that he had been sated.

She felt a wash of anger come over her. He grinned. "Turnabout's fair play, sweetheart. I'll try not to leave you burning as long as you did me."

She gasped. He kissed her chin, her neck, the

space between her breasts. He tugged at one of the tassels. "Shall these stay or go?"

Apparently, he asked himself that question, for he didn't listen to her answer. Holding the tassel with just enough pressure to lift her nipple, he nuzzled the underside of her breast, then repeated that torture with her other breast.

Addy rubbed her hands over his broad shoulders and bulky arms, easing her hands up to his face, holding him in place. It didn't keep him still. He nuzzled the stretchy lace of her bodysuit as he made his way down her chest, over her stomach, to her mound.

The bodysuit came with a pair of attached panties that opened at the crotch and only had front coverage. Owen knelt on the floor at the foot of the bed and pulled her down to the edge of the mattress. Spreading her legs, he explored the fabric and the places it exposed on her body. She gasped when his fingers touched her clit, and then his mouth was there, sucking, stroking, working her into a fever of need. Each time she almost came, he'd slow down.

"Owen! Now!" She fisted the bedspread, unable to arch up against him, since he was holding her hips up. He stood between her legs and, still holding her hips where he wanted them, entered her, hard and hot and so rigid, filling her. His hips pumped as he pounded into her. She cried out, begging him for more, for everything, for all of him. He changed his hold to one arm under her hips, freeing a hand to play with her clit. She lost whatever control she had remaining over her own body. Ecstasy took her. She was aware at some level that Owen had come with her, but the echoes of her release lasted longer than his.

When it was over, she was done. Empty and yet restored. He lifted her up to the pillows, settling to her on top of the bedspread. It was dark in the room—the only light came from the overhead hallway light between the closet and bathroom. It was enough to let her see the intense look on his face.

She smiled up at him. "What is it?"

"Did I hurt you?"

"Of course not. You never would." She touched his face, hoping to ease some of the tightness she saw. "Did I torture you too much?"

"No. Just right. What made you think of this?" He nodded at her sexy bodysuit.

"The girls and I were talking about having a bachelorette party. I was worried they might be partied out, with Thanksgiving and then Christmas and then Max and Hope's wedding. Some of them came up with the idea of having a fuckfest."

Owen's brows lifted. "Fuckfest? Who suggest—Never mind. I don't want to know."

"They thought it was funny imagining you losing your control."

"Oh, did they?"

"Yeah, but the really funny thing was seeing them

trying to sex me up. I've been pretty shut down in that area since I was abducted."

He rolled over to his side and braced his head on his hand. "So how did they 'sex you up'?"

"Remember when we took over the game room and locked you guys out? Well, we were brainstorming what to do for the wedding. Things got a little raunchy." She felt a little sad revealing what she told the girls, but maybe it was time that he knew. "I told them that I sometimes wished you'd lose control, that sometimes I feel you're too careful of me."

"Well, yeah. I love you. You've been through hell and back. I don't want to take from you more than you can give."

"But that's just it. Sometimes your carefulness reminds me of all that happened, all that's between us."

"I don't mean for it to do that."

"I know. But that's when the girls started brainstorming how I could push you over the edge, break through your control."

He circled the soft flesh of one breast, moving around the pasty that was still affixed to her nipple. "I'd say you accomplished that goal tonight."

She nodded, feeling rather pleased with herself. "I did, didn't I? They pulled up some sexy lingerie sites, then somehow we all started watching porn in the hopes that I might learn some moves."

Owen laughed, and Addy could feel herself

turning bright red. She wondered what color her eyes were at the moment.

"You watched porn?" he asked, shocked.

"I did. They knew sites that mostly featured female enjoyment. It wasn't awful. In fact, I kind of enjoyed it."

"They've corrupted my innocent soon-to-be-wife."

She hit his shoulder. "I'm a long way from innocent. Do you hate me?"

His brow wrinkled. "Hell no. You want to try something, I'm all in. Not sure I'd go for full-on role playing, but a new position, a new toy, some temporary rules, sure."

"I love you."

He kissed her forehead. "I love you. Thank you for tonight. I was wondering where our kids were."

"We worked that out, too. Troy is having a sleepover with Zavi, and Augie is with the pride. Wynn was keeping them all in the movie room so they wouldn't see when you lost control."

"You girls had this all figured out, huh?"

She fought a guilty grin. "Maybe."

"For the record, I didn't lose control. I got exactly what I wanted. You. No walls. No fears. No worries. Just a straight line to your soul." He rolled over, lifting her on top of him. "Since this is our fuckfest, and the night's still early, I'm sure we have several more fun things we can do while you're wearing that outfit." He entered her, watching her in the soft light.

Addy moved over him, her hands on his ripped abdomen. Sometimes it really was a shock knowing he was hers now, forever, after all the hell they'd both been through. They had the new beginning she'd yearned for. "You did lose control, Owen."

He grinned. "Maybe I did. Just a little."

"Just a lot, or you wouldn't have carried me from the dining room."

"What's your point?"

"I win."

He started thrusting in her. "I think we both win."

## 9

Saturday dawned a dark and snowy day. Addy caught the delicious scent of coffee before opening her eyes. Even better than having coffee in bed was the gorgeous man bringing it to her. He grinned as her eyes focused on him.

"Morning," Owen said.

Addy stretched and smiled. "Morning."

"Would my almost-wife like some coffee?"

"Your almost-wife would kill for a cup. Or three." She pushed herself up just as Troy ran into the room. His brown hair was tousled and his feet were bare, but he already wore his wedding suit. He crawled up next to her. She and Owen exchanged smiles.

"I see you're already set for the wedding," Addy said.

"I am. I'm the ring bearer, Mom."

"I know. But the wedding isn't until this afternoon. You can't wear that until then."

"But this is a big day."

"It is. And I promise you won't miss it if you wear play clothes until later."

"I'm the *only* ring bearer, right?"

"You are."

"Good."

"Why?" Owen asked.

"'Cause Zavi wanted to be one, too, but I said he couldn't be."

"Why can't he?"

"Because *I'm* your son. I want to bring both rings."

Just then Zavi, also already in his suit, hurried into their room. He climbed on the bed and gave Troy a dark look. Addy sent Owen a glance, catching his raised brows and a smile he tried to hide.

"Good morning, Zavi," Addy said.

"Morning, Aunt Addy." He rubbed his eyes as his bottom lip quivered.

"Did you have some breakfast?" she asked.

"No. Troy said I can't be a ring bearer today. But I have a suit. And I already did it once, so I know how to do it. He hasn't done it before."

"You aren't their son," Troy said. "I am."

Zavi looked crushed. He got off the bed and slowly crossed the room, his little shoulders slumped. Addy sent Owen a silent plea, hoping he'd find a solution.

Owen put his coffee mug on the nightstand then sat on the edge of the bed. "Zavi, come here." Zavi did, but he was heaving ragged breaths as he tried not to cry. Owen lifted him up onto his leg. "Troy, you too." He lifted Troy onto the opposite leg. "You boys are friends, right?"

"Yeah," Troy said.

"Your friend's hurting, Troy. We don't leave our friends hurting. Is there something you could do to help him feel better?"

Zavi sniffled and swiped at a tear.

Troy glared at him. "I'll be nice to him at the wedding."

"You should always be nice to your friends."

"He can't be a ring bearer. We don't have two pillows."

"I'm sure we can find another small pillow in this huge house."

Zavi looked so sad—Addy had no idea how her son could deny him. She sipped her coffee, then ventured into the fray. "Troy, wouldn't it be nice to share your big day with your friend? Sometimes friends are few and far between. Today's a day you'll both remember for a long time—and that makes it even more special."

"We could go try to find another pillow," Zavi suggested.

"Okay," Troy said. "If we can find one, then we can both do it. I think I know where we can get one." They got off Owen's knees. Troy put his arm around Zavi's shoulders as they walked to the door. "I'm sorry I made you cry."

Zavi shrugged as another ragged breath left his chest. "It's okay." They left the room.

Owen chuckled and leaned across the bed. He grinned as he reached for Addy's hand. "First catastrophe of the day averted."

Addy smiled. "I'm so happy."

"You ready for this?"

"I am."

"Do you have your vows memorized?"

"I do, but I'm bringing them on paper anyway just in case I get flustered. How about you?"

"They're all in here." He touched his chest. "I can't forget them."

Everything Owen said and did drew him deeper into her heart. He treated her and her boys as if he cherished them. "I'm so glad you never found someone else to love. I know that's selfish of me, but—"

Owen shook his head. "No, it's not. You're my great love, Addy. No one else compared. No one ever could." He stood up. "Now let's go have breakfast before they hide you away, and I have to be without you for hours."

"Hey—Case," Lion gestured to the limp sides of the tie draped over his neck. "Can you help?"

Casey's heart squeezed to the point of breaking. "Sure."

They were alone in the little alcove that led out to the gym wing. Casey gave him a quick smile, then got to work. Better to finish quickly and get away from him before she embarrassed herself. Unfortunately, neither her hands nor the tie cooperated. Her first attempt was a mess, and she had to pull it all apart and start over.

He frowned. "You okay?" he asked.

"Yeah, why?"

"You don't seem yourself."

She licked her lips, trying to drag herself away from the cliff she was standing on. He was a man. She was girl. How much clearer could her mom have made their differences?

"I miss you." There. She'd said it. The truth. The whole truth, and everything it held within. He'd only been gone a week, and already her heart was like a puppy dropped off on the side of the road. She could feel heat climbing up her neck.

He tilted his head. "You're pretty when you do that." His lips twisted into a half-grin. "You're always pretty, but I like it when you blush. It's like your face blooms."

Her eyes watered. She blinked to clear them. "Do you think the next eight years will go fast?"

His brows lifted. The scrolling lines of the tattoos above his eyes were only partly obscured by his naturally tawny brows; she stared at them instead of his eyes.

"I hope not," he said. "I'm looking forward to

every moment of them." He frowned. "Why did you ask that?"

She shrugged. She finished his tie and forced her hands away from him. "I guess I'm not looking forward to all the years of school and college that I have left." *...Before we can be together.* Did he read between the lines? Had she said too much?

He smiled. "I guess that part will go quickly. Especially if you make it fun."

How could it be fun without him?

"That's what I intend to do," he said. He gestured toward the door. "Ready to go in?"

"Not yet. I'm running some errands for my mom to help Addy."

"Okay. Catch you inside."

A KNOCK SOUNDED on Addy's door, then it opened. She froze, worried Owen would see her before the ceremony, but it was Troy's little face that popped around the door. He and Augie came inside.

"Hi, Mom," Augie said. "We just wanted to come by and—" He stopped and stared at her. "Wow. You look great."

Troy ran up and hugged her hips. She held her arm out for Augie to join them. "Thanks, honey. You know what's best about today? I get to have both of you at my wedding. I can't think of anything better than that."

"You can't?" Wendell asked as he came into the room. "What about having your brother there to hold your bouquet?"

Addy laughed. "Well, that too!"

"We've been staying with Dad, doing boy stuff so you could do your girl stuff," Troy said. "Are you finished yet? Everyone's downstairs waiting."

"Are they?" Addy looked over at Wendell to confirm.

"Well, everyone except for the female half of the group, who are all here," Wendell said, nodding toward the women sitting on the chairs and bed.

"I guess that's our cue to head down," Mandy said as she lifted herself out of one of the chairs in Owen's room. She gave Addy a hug and made a little adjustment on her hair. It was pulled up at the sides and fell behind her head in wide curls, with a froth of baby's-breath for decoration.

Ace snapped a picture of that moment. One by one, each of the ladies gave Addy a hug then slipped out of the room.

"Jax, take the boys out to the sitting room," Ace said. "I want a last word with Addy."

Addy smiled at Ace, hoping to ease the tension in her friend's face. She took Ace's hands. "You don't have to say anything."

"I do. We've been in this spot before. I could have —should have—stopped it before."

"No, you couldn't have. You were barely older than Augie is now. And we were never in this spot.

Today is filled with hope and joy. It's the only day like it I've ever known."

Ace nodded. "I hope that we can be friends, Addy."

"We are friends. All of us. No matter what happens, we're family."

Ace nodded. "I like that." She hugged Addy, then lifted her camera. "I'm going to go ahead of you so that I can get some candid shots of your procession."

When she left, Addy took a last look at her reflection. Her dress was a tea-length white satin overlaid with guipure lace in a floral pattern. The fitted bodice had a sweetheart shape with narrow off-the-shoulders sleeves. A wide satin ribbon wrapped around the waist for a big bow in the back of the dress. The flaring skirt was made possible with several layers of stiff crinoline underskirts. She loved it and couldn't wait to see Owen's expression. She'd been shocked that Val's friend had had just the right dress for her based on the pics she'd had Val send in. Maybe one day, she'd have a daughter who might wear it to her wedding.

A knock sounded on the door. "I'm coming, Wendell!" she called out as she hurried over.

"It's me," Owen's deep voice came through the door.

"No! You can't see me. Owen!"

"Addy, I need to."

She set her hand on the door. "Why?"

"I have a gift for you."

"Owen, you can't come in."

"Then I'll send Augie in with it."

Addy stepped back as the door opened. Augie slipped inside, quickly followed by Troy. Their eyes were happy. Augie handed her a long, narrow box.

"Owen, what is this?" she asked, letting her voice carry through the cracked door.

"A gift. I want you to wear it today. Please."

Addy's hands shook as she ripped off the wrapping. She looked at her boys before opening the box.

"Hurry, Mom," Augie urged.

She flipped the case open and gasped. There, lying on black velvet, was a bracelet of aquamarines and diamond baguettes that alternated the entire length.

"Oh my God. This is gorgeous."

"You like it?" Owen asked.

"I love it."

"Have Augie put it on you."

She handed him the bracelet then held her hand out. He snapped it around her wrist.

"It's beautiful, Mom," Troy said, gently touching it.

"I love you, Owen."

"I love you too. C'mon, boys. We need to get downstairs."

Both boys hugged her. She waited for them to leave the sitting room. "Is it safe, Wendell?"

"All clear," he replied. "Ready to do this?"

"I am so ready."

He held her hand as they walked down the hall.

Outside the gym, they faced each other, pausing for a moment. Her brother's expression was heartbreakingly serious.

"I love you, sis." His words were heavy with so many things spoken only by his eyes.

She smiled. "I love you, Wendelly."

He nodded. "Shall we go in?"

"Yes!" She laughed.

The doors to the gym opened for them, held by Kelan and Ty. They both gave her fortifying smiles and seemed as happy as she was.

There was a big area between the door and the altar. Despite their practice walk during the rehearsal, Addy suddenly wanted to run forward. Wendell held her to a slow space. She caught Owen's gaze. He solemnly held his hand on his heart.

"Jesus, does that man love you," her brother whispered.

Addy's heart beat a fierce rhythm.

Wendell handed her off to Owen, then took his place behind her. She reached over and handed him her bouquet, which he took with a wry smile.

Owen reached for her hands. She was grateful his grip was so steady and firm. His pale eyes held hers captive, reminding her that she was here, with him, at this new step in their lives. His thumb brushed across the backs of her hands.

"You are so beautiful," Owen whispered as he kissed her forehead.

"Beloved family and friends, we're gathered here

today… Oh, heck. I suppose you all know we're here to witness an important evolution in Owen and Addy's relationship."

Addy smiled at the officiant's change in delivery.

"They've known each other since they were children, playing imaginary games and sharing chickenpox. As often happens, their lives didn't unfold in the way they'd hoped. Time and terrible experiences separated them, but despite the years, despite the pain of their separation, love brought them back together. And it is in the name of love that today we witness their lives forever united.

"Owen and Addy, a marriage isn't simply created in a mere ceremony. It is a living, breathing event that lasts the rest of your lives. It takes careful tending so that it may rise above simply existing to a state where it thrives.

"Owen, do you take Addy as your wife, a life partner to be cherished? Do you accept her as your equal in all things? Will you honor her, protect her, be faithful to her as long as you both shall live?"

Owen's lips tilted in a half-smile. "I do." He then mouthed, *Fuck yeah*. His eyes were so intense, she almost melted on the spot.

"Addy, do you take Owen as your husband, a life partner to be cherished? Do you accept him as your equal in all things? Will you honor him, protect him, be faithful to him as long as you both shall live?"

Owen arched a brow at her. She almost laughed. "I do."

"Owen and Addy, beyond the words I've said and your intent which brought us here today, you have vows to say to each other. Catch them in your hearts and never let go of them." The officiant nodded to Owen.

"Addy, I've always known that I loved you," Owen began. "It wasn't easy waiting for you to also realize we were one person in two bodies. And even when I thought I'd lost you, you were my one and only. I will spend my life making your life everything you wish it to be. I look forward to all we'll experience and build together. I can't believe we get another chance, and I vow I will not waste a single moment of our time."

The tears in his eyes were almost Addy's undoing. She reached up on her tiptoes and kissed his cheek. "I love you."

"I love you."

Addy squared her shoulders. Turned out she didn't need her written lines after all. She just needed to speak her truth. "Owen, silly man, I knew when I was born that you were mine and I was yours. Why do you think I always cast you as my knight in shining armor and sent you out to battle my dragons, and, well, my brother?" Owen smiled at her. "It seems we've lived three lifetimes already. Before the hell. The hell. And now this heaven. In each, you were my beacon of light. I know the world will change, and I know we'll change with it. I vow to always love you, always honor you, and to strive to become your beacon of light."

"You are that light, Addy," Owen assured her.

"Owen and Addy, you've chosen to exchange rings during your ceremony," the officiant said. "Let us consider the symbolism of a ring, a circle, a thing often thought to have no beginning and no end. But everything has a beginning and an end, marriage included. Your rings were made from raw materials that came from the earth and were transformed into something polished and beautiful. So too will your life as a married couple be forged in the fires of sorrow and joy. You were raw and separate before today united you. And you will spend the rest of your lives polishing and forming your beautiful marriage.

"Troy, please hold the pillow with your father's ring on it for your mother." The officiant nodded when Troy moved to stand next to Addy. Addy smiled and stroked her hand over his head. "Zavi, please hold the pillow with your aunt's ring for your uncle to take." Zavi grinned up at Owen as he moved to stand next to him.

"Owen, please place the ring on Addy's finger and repeat these words after me."

Addy stared into Owen's eyes as he pushed the ring just to her knuckle, then, in his deep voice, repeated what the officiant said. "Addy, I give you this ring as a sign that I choose you to be my wife and best friend to the end of my days."

Addy sniffled. When she was directed, she took the ring Troy held on the little pillow. Her hand shook as she pushed it to Owen's knuckle. "Owen, I give you this ring as a sign that I choose you to be my husband and best friend to the end of my days."

Owen's smile was blinding. She barely heard the next words their officiant said.

"I've presided over many weddings in my career. Some of them here." He chuckled. "Owen, Addy, the vows you've exchanged here today are sacred to your souls. May I add my own wishes for your union? Two simple things.

"Remember to always strive for kindness in your interactions. Be uplifting to each other and your home will always be a place of refuge for you and your loved ones.

"Love lavishly. I don't mean living beyond your means. I mean laugh easily, compliment each other often, and always reach for joy. Make your marriage the richest experience you'll ever have."

Addy and Owen nodded.

"Then, ladies and gentlemen, I am delighted to present to you your beloved friends, Owen and Addy, now Mr. and Mrs. Tremaine. You may now share your first kiss."

Addy was laughing and crying as Owen's warm mouth met hers. When they separated, a little cloud of confetti snowed down over them. Addy knelt to hug Troy and Zavi, then reached for Augie.

Troy knelt down to scoop up as much confetti as he could and throw it again. Zavi did that too. Both boys laughed then hugged. Everyone closed in around Addy and Owen, but she looked back at her boys in time to see Augie move over next to Troy and set a hand on his shoulder.

Wendell came over and hugged them both. He still held her bouquet. She laughed and reached for it. "Maybe I should take that again—unless you're enjoying it."

"Yes. Take it. Thank God." He kissed her cheek again as he handed it to her. The event staff were moving the chairs off the dance floor and returning them to the tables.

Everything progressed in the orderly fashion that the wedding planner had mapped out for them, but it was mostly a blur for Addy—until the music started and Owen bowed in front of her, offering her his hand.

She took it and smiled at him, seeing in her mind the lonely man he'd been, writing about his lost dreams to a dead woman. And now they were together, married, making their dreams come true.

# 10

_____

Selena carried her bag downstairs. It was late, past midnight. Owen, Jax, and Nick were waiting for her. She nodded at Owen, afraid to get close enough to shake hands for fear of what Bastion would do to him.

She felt numb. The effort of blocking Bastion from her mind meant she had to block everything—all emotions, memories, hopes, and fears. She could not think, could not remember, and could not feel anything without giving all of that away to the man who was stalking her.

It would be so much easier to do if she didn't have to fight herself as well—she wanted to share everything she was with him. She yearned to see him and talk to him. He laughed easily, and it was fun teasing him.

But he was a danger to the team, and she would lay down her life before causing any of them harm.

Leaving here was a good plan. If he were only seducing her to get to them, then he'd soon give up on her.

But if he was serious about her, then all bets were off. The team was risking everything on this chance.

She was surprised to see the rest of the team waiting for her on the patio. They separated into two groups that she had to walk between. Ace looked furious; Selena knew she'd argued her case to come with her and had been denied. She didn't hug Ace—or anyone. She didn't want to lose her composure—again. The numbness she was forcing on herself could only be held in place with extreme effort. She nodded at everyone, then crossed the lawn to the helicopter. Jax and Nick followed her onboard.

Nick handed her a blindfold. "Just a precaution. Don't want anyone to find your location based on your observations of your surroundings."

Selena connected a pair of sound-cancelling headphones to a playlist on her phone, then wrapped the blindfold around her eyes and tied it tight. She covered her ears with the headphones, then leaned back in her seat, trying not to focus on the turns she felt or the amount of time that passed. No doubt the pilot was taking turns that weren't needed for a straight trip to their destination, and so the time and direction they took wouldn't be indicative of their destination.

She could feel Bastion with her, pushing in at the edges of her mind, trying to get inside. He was desperate to get to her—she could feel that in him, almost to the point of pain. But was that because of her, or because she'd just shut off his access to the team? The harder he pushed, the harder she forced her mind to focus only on her own breathing and the mind-numbing rhythms of her music.

As if any of that mattered. They were practically different species. She had no future with a man like him. He had to know that.

She realized that was her answer. He wanted what he was after—and that wasn't her. She'd just been his tool.

Fuck it all. She was tired of being used by men.

Hours later, they reached their destination. She removed her headphones and was about to remove the blindfold, but Jax stopped her.

"Leave it on, Sel," Jax said as he leaned close to speak over the roar of the helicopter. "The less Bastion can see of where we are, the better."

"I'm not staying blindfolded here."

"No, of course not. But for a few days, let's limit your exposure to the property. Maybe he'll give up and abandon using you. One week max."

They disembarked, stepping out into brutally cold weather and wind that raked exposed skin. Someone handed her bag to her. She tossed the strap over her head. Nick and Jax took an arm each and led her quickly down a hill. They crossed a long, flat stretch of snow-covered ground.

"Some steps now," Jax said as they climbed about

a dozen stairs. Selena heard a heavy door creak as it opened.

"Good evening, sir," a man said.

The door closed behind them, making a heavy echo. Selena reached up for her blindfold and removed it.

A man she didn't know greeted her with a slight bow and a warm smile. "I'm Spencer Hudson, butler here and part of Mr. Jacobs' security staff. I'll show you to your room, if you're ready."

Selena nodded at Jax and Nick, refusing to let them see how unsettled she was. She forced that—and all—emotion from her mind as she strived for full-on neutral and followed the butler up a wide set of marble stairs.

"GREER—A WORD, PLEASE," Owen said as the sound of the helicopter faded away. They walked to the den, where Owen closed the door behind them. What he was about to ask sounded crazy as hell. "I need you to do something."

"Name it." Greer didn't even flinch.

"Ask Blade if he has some old bear traps. They aren't uncommon on ranches like this. If he doesn't, I need you to source some. Two or three."

"Okay. We hunting bears now?"

"I want two set up outside the tunnel entrance to the bunker. The other I want placed in the path this thing most frequently takes on his way to the house."

Greer was silent.

"You got a problem with that directive?"

"No."

"It's non-lethal and non-digital. I don't want you to discuss this with anyone other than Blade, and then only where no one else can hear you. Selena is not to know about it. Don't put in an online order if he doesn't have traps here."

"Our online traffic is secure."

"I don't believe it."

"I do. Max and I built our infrastructure."

"We have no idea what this thing is capable of, and until we do, nothing is secure."

"This thing has a name."

Owen narrowed his eyes. "I want Bastion caught."

"Copy that. I will need to let Max know about the traps because he stores his and Hope's bikes in the tunnel."

Owen gave a curt nod. "Only him and Blade, though."

SELENA MADE the mistake of sleeping deeply—a luxury she'd resisted for the weeks she'd been here. She dreamt about a wedding. Hers. But for some reason, she was late to the ceremony. When she tried to get into the venue, all the doors were locked. She knocked and knocked, but no one came to let her in. She went around the side of the building and looked in a window. There was Bastion, dancing with another woman.

She woke abruptly, angry and sad and shaking.

The thing she feared the most had come to pass—she was alone, because of *him*.

*Where are you?* Bastion's voice whispered through her mind. He sounded angry.

She'd been working on blocking him from her mind ever since she'd gotten there. *I don't know*, she answered.

*Talk to me. I will find you.*

*I don't want you to.* But she did want that. Terribly. In part so that she could stop fighting herself. And in part because she'd missed having him just a thought away.

*Yes, you do. I can feel your pain.*

*Can you feel everyone's pain?*

*Only yours…and my brothers'.*

*Do you have a lot of them?*

*Yes. Please, let me come to you.*

*You can't use me anymore*, Selena said.

*I never did use you.*

*You asked me to get info on the Ratcliffs.*

*A favor. For a friend. They have information we desperately need, but I don't care about any of that. Tell me where you are.*

*I don't know. It hurts, Bastion, keeping you out.*

*It's because we are carved from the same soul, and having found our other half, we cannot exist apart.*

*I don't believe in souls.*

*I do.*

Selena tried to block a sob, but it broke free. She covered her face with a pillow, but it was no match for Bastion, since he was already in her head...and maybe in her heart. *I wish you were here.*

*Don't block me. I will find you.*

AN ALERT SOUNDED in the ops room. Greer checked it then looked at Max. It had been weeks since Owen had ordered him to set out the traps. "He's coming."

"From where?" Max asked.

"The side of the house leading to the tunnel entrance."

Max gave Greer a ruthless grin, then stood and checked his pistol. "Let's go greet him."

They went into the tunnel. Motion lights turned on as they progressed through it. Instead of placing the traps at the tunnel entrance, they'd put them in the tunnel itself. Harder to avoid that way.

They stopped just in front of the traps and waited. Lights switched on at the other end of the tunnel and continued switching on as something moved forward, coming toward them.

Greer was surprised that Bastion didn't try to hide himself. He could have blown the lights, but he didn't. At first, Greer could only see Bastion's silhouette. It grew larger as he approached. He was a tall man, broad-shouldered, and moved in a fluid, athletic way.

Bastion came within feet of Greer and Max before stopping. "Where is she?" he asked.

He spoke with a heavy French accent. Up close, he did look like the Captain Hook that Troy had seen.

"She's gone," Greer said.

"Where?"

"She's not your concern," Max said.

Bastion's head slowly turned his way. His eyes went from dark brown to a glowing gold. "I will end you and everyone in this house, soul by soul, until I learn where she's gone."

"Not true." Greer waved that off. "You're a soldier, like us. You follow orders. If you'd been ordered to kill us, we'd already be dead, given your abilities. So what's your interest in her?"

Bastion's burning eyes turned to him. A dull ache began in Greer's head. He winced and checked to see if Max was feeling the same thing. The ache became a sound, a deep, terrible sound, like something just at the edges of a sonic boom.

Max hit his knees.

"Enough!" Greer shouted as he bent over. The pain was so intense, it took everything he had not to vomit. "Enough!"

The pain ended.

Greer gasped at the relief, still holding his knees. He looked up at Bastion. "If there's something you want, meet with us. Let's talk about it."

"You took my woman," Bastion said through clenched teeth.

Max shook his head and slowly straightened. "She's ours not yours." He and Greer moved back a step.

Bastion stepped forward, right into the bear trap. He screamed and stumbled forward, into the teeth of the second trap.

An explosion of some sort broke free, blowing Greer and Max back several yards. It seemed they'd just hit the dirt when the rest of the team spilled into the tunnel around them. Greer shook his head and pushed to his feet, searching for Bastion.

The traps were there, but he was gone.

# OTHER BOOKS BY ELAINE LEVINE

(This series may be read in any order)

# ABOUT THE AUTHOR

Elaine Levine lives in the mountains of Colorado with her husband and a rescued pit bull/bull mastiff mix. In addition to writing the Red Team romantic suspense series, she's the author of several books in the historical western romance series Men of Defiance. She also has a novel in the multi-author series, Sleeper SEALs.

Be sure to sign up for her new release announcements at http://geni.us/GAlUjx.

If you enjoyed this book, please consider leaving a review at your favorite online retailer to help other readers find it.

Get social! Connect with Elaine online:
    Reader Group: http://geni.us/2w5d
    Website: https://www.ElaineLevine.com
    email: elevine@elainelevine.com

Made in the USA
Monee, IL
20 November 2019